Nice Work If You Can Get It . . .

"The Pit is the spot where we work. Long time ago some old fool prospector discovered gold down there and now it's a full-bore mine," said Eli.

"Filled with, let me guess, slaves doing the digging," said Slocum.

"Yeah, you're a sharp knife, all right."

Knife, thought Slocum. They must have hit me hard, or I would have remembered my boot knife before now. He tried to work his bound hands down closer to his boots, with no such luck in sight. "So they tell me. Why is it called the Pit?"

"'Cause that's what it is—a big pit with tunnels shooting off of it. But there's two problems with it: One, it's a ravine, a canyon with no way out."

"If there's a way in," said Slocum, who finally managed to heave himself upright and lean against the wall of the darkened room, "then there's a way out."

"It ain't that easy," said Eli. "But you'll see soon enough."

Slocum breathed deeply, trying to gather his fuzzy wits. "You mentioned two problems. What's the second?"

"Oh yeah, the Pit? It's filled with rattlesnakes."

A-14

JAKE LOGAN

SLOCUM
AND THE
SNAKE-PIT SLAVERS

J

JOVE BOOKS, NEW YORK

THE BERKLEY PUBLISHING GROUP
Published by the Penguin Group
Penguin Group (USA) Inc.
375 Hudson Street, New York, New York 10014, USA

USA I Canada I UK I Ireland I Australia I New Zealand I India I South Africa I China

Penguin Books Ltd., Registered Offices: 80 Strand, London WC2R 0RL, England
For more information about the Penguin Group, visit penguin.com.

SLOCUM AND THE SNAKE-PIT SLAVERS

A Jove Book / published by arrangement with the author

Jove Books are published by The Berkley Publishing Group.
JOVE® is a registered trademark of Penguin Group (USA) Inc.
The "J" design is a trademark of Penguin Group (USA) Inc.

For information, address: The Berkley Publishing Group,
a division of Penguin Group (USA) Inc.,
375 Hudson Street, New York, New York 10014.

ISBN: 978-0-515-15314-9

PUBLISHING HISTORY
Jove mass-market edition / June 2013

PRINTED IN THE UNITED STATES OF AMERICA

10 9 8 7 6 5 4 3 2 1

Cover illustration by Sergio Giovine.

1

"Who are you?"

John Slocum spun at the sound, trough water running off his face, dripping from his hair. He sluiced the water from his eyes with one hand as he snatched his Colt Navy from its holster with the other.

There before him stood an old scowling Mexican. He wore shapeless peasant trousers and a shirt that had once been white, cinched in the middle by a frayed woven belt of brown hemp, knotted double in the middle, harnessing a too-thin waist. But it was the business end of the double-bore shotgun that got Slocum's attention.

"Wasn't sure anybody was around here. Seemed almost abandoned."

The man's scowl didn't flinch; neither did the gun. His eyes were shaded by the tatty brim of an old palm sombrero.

Slocum wasn't about to lower his Colt, even if he could only see out of one eye, the other still stinging with sweat and running with the tepid water he'd scooped on himself from the trough.

"I came by this way looking for Marybeth Meecher. She used to run this roadhouse. She around?" He didn't think she was any longer, judging by the run-down condition of the place, but it had suddenly become important to him to get some sort of answer out of this scowling fellow. Still no response.

Slocum ground his teeth. Curse me for a fool for letting the heat get the better of my senses. Beside him the Appaloosa kept on drinking. You'd think they'd been a week adrift in the Sonora Desert and not ranging wide and free in the high mountains of Wyoming Territory.

"You going to shoot me or just try to kill me with that hard stare?"

"You got no business here."

"And you do?" Something about the man, maybe an edge of fear in his voice, told Slocum any danger he thought he might be in was now winking out like a blown candle. He slowly holstered his pistol, not taking his eyes off the Mexican for a second. He wasn't mistaken when he saw relief play over the dark man's cragged features.

"You aren't supposed to be here."

"I could say the same thing to you," said Slocum, settling his sweat-stained hat back on his head, tugging the brim low. "Except I don't know just where here is anymore."

The Mexican tried to resurrect his scowl, but evidently decided that Slocum looked harmless. "You talk funny, mister."

The old man lowered the shotgun, but Slocum noticed that the man kept his callused fingers cradling tight to the worn butternut stock of the well-tended weapon.

"Again, I could say the same thing, but what would the point be?" Slocum tugged the bandanna from his back pocket and finished drying his face. "What I meant is . . . what happened to this place? It sure has changed since the last time I was through here a couple of years back."

"You been here?" The man squinted, leaned forward, studying Slocum's face. "Yes, yes, I remember you now."

"You remember me?" Slocum cocked his head. "Funny, your face doesn't look familiar to me."

"You were here almost three years ago."

"Yeah, could well be three, now that you mention it. But when I was here, this place was in better shape." Slocum nodded toward the low building before him, its boards popped and gray with weather and age, tumbleweeds choking the corral. "What happened here? This place was run by the nice young woman I mentioned before, Miss Marybeth Meecher."

"*Sí*, she was good to me—like family." The man let the shotgun slump all the way now, his forearms corded by its heavy weight.

"What do you mean, 'was'?"

The creases of the man's lined face deepened further. "Some people, local Indians, they come three months ago, and they and Miss Meecher, they talk long into the night."

"What were they talking about?"

"About the men from the ranch. Only they don't deserve to be talked about with the same mouth as Miss Meecher. She was good to me."

"I see, yeah. We've been down that path already. Is Miss Meecher safe? What, exactly, are you trying to tell me?"

The swarthy man sighed. "They are not good men. But Miss Meecher . . . she is away just now. She will be back one day soon."

"Great. Now that we've established that there are bad men about and Miss Meecher is the salt of the earth and she's gone missing, I should ask you one thing."

"*Sí?*"

Slocum mounted his horse and toed his right boot into the stirrup. "What am I still doing talking to you?"

"*Que?*"

"Miss Meecher was, is, a friend of mine. If you can't tell me what has happened to her, then I'll find someone who can. Maybe north of here. I have a job waiting for me up in the Absarokas anyway, and if I don't get there soon, I'm sunk before I float. So if you'll excuse me, you're just going to have to tend to things here without a new conversation partner." He touched his hat brim and angled the Appaloosa between the staring man and the water trough. "Maybe a stage will come along. Who knows? You might find a few eager ears on it."

Slocum tapped spur to the Appaloosa's belly and cantered northward up the dusty lane. He was half tempted to look back, knowing what he'd see—the old Mexican standing there before the ill-kept way station, shotgun drooped, that sagged, hangdog look on his face. The man had seemed as if he'd been playing hard at the game of life for a long, long time and had only recently realized he'd been beat at it years before, just hadn't known it.

Slocum almost made it to the near bend in the lane when the man's voice reached him: "Hey! You headed to the Triple T Ranch, no?"

Slocum closed his eyes and sighed, then reined up. How in the hell did this man know where he was headed? All he'd told him was that he had a job at a ranch in the Absarokas. The last time he'd been up that way, there were several ranches in that region.

He sighed again for good measure and guided the horse around, then sat there staring at the man. Yep, looked just about like he'd expected him to. Still sagged. But dammit if the old coot didn't have a smile on his face. "Just how in the hell did you know that?" shouted Slocum.

"Ah, Miguel always knows things. Sometimes they are useful things, sometimes not. But this time, I figure this is a useful thing, no?"

"No." Slocum shook his head. "I doubt that your guess is much of a useful thing at all."

"But you are not looking for work at the Triple T Ranch?"

"Maybe . . ."

"Well, you won't find it there, mister. At least not good work."

Slocum sighed again. It seemed like the right thing to do.

He swung the Appaloosa around and made his way back to the little Mexican. As he did, he swore he caught movement out of the corner of his eye, just inside the curtained window of the front room of the place. "Where did you say Miss Meecher was anyway?"

"I didn't say."

"Why not?"

"Because I don't know. But she'll be back soon."

"Well now, how do you know that if you don't know where she went?"

"I just know, that's all."

"How long ago did she leave?"

The man shrugged. An exasperated growl came from the dark building behind him. The Mexican's face tensed and he stared hard at Slocum, but he didn't turn around.

"What was that? You keeping pigs in there?"

"What? No, no. No pigs in the house."

"Because it sure sounded like a pig or some sort of rooting beast in there."

Before the old man could protest further, the slab-wood door burst open and banged back on its strap-leather hinges. A barefoot young woman stepped out, rage sparking her wide, almond-shaped eyes. Her long, raven hair, blue-black and glinting in the afternoon sun, swung free about her shoulders. Her full red lips were pulled into a hard line, and her delicate nostrils flexed in anger.

She was dressed in a long flowered skirt, well worn but clean and in good repair. Her once-red shirt wrapped about her lithe form as bark clings to a wiry sapling. Her full breasts bore out the fact that this demure dynamo was closer to a woman than a girl.

Slocum took in all this with a quick glance, but had time for little more because the old Mexican spun on her, pointing back toward the house and unleashing a flurry of stinging words in the fastest Mexican lingo Slocum had ever heard. The girl was having none of it, however, and stalked around him. As she stomped closer to Slocum, her breasts bounced with each step, and Slocum found himself momentarily transfixed.

"Ma'am." He touched his hat.

"Pig, is it? Pig? You call me a pig?"

"I did no such thing." He dismounted and poked his hat brim, tipping the hat back on his head. This day was getting more interesting by the second.

"But I did happen to notice someone—or some *thing* in the house. Thought I might try to lure it out."

She stopped before him, hands on her hips, her ample chest heaving.

"And it worked," he said, smiling. His smile had just reached full width when her right hand lashed upward and caught him full on his left cheek. It stung but not enough to wipe the smile from his face. She gritted her perfect white teeth and lashed upward again. This time he caught her wrist and she growled in renewed anger.

"I'll thank you kindly not to strike me, ma'am. Not at least until we've hand a chance to become better acquainted."

"Tita, please. This is no way to treat a stranger." The old man looked at Slocum. "Besides, I think"—he looked toward his worn boots—"I think he is a good man, no?" He looked back at Slocum hopefully.

The girl relaxed in Slocum's grip.

"I'd like to think I'm a . . . good man," he said, his smile leveling out to a serious gaze. "Now, want to tell me what this is all about?"

The girl still looked as if she wanted to peel Slocum's head off and stomp it in the dirt like a rotten tomatillo. But there was something else there, too—a hint of a smile, perhaps, around those dark, devilish eyes.

"Come in," said the old man. "We can at least prepare a meal for you. We were about to eat, so it is only right that we break bread with a traveler. Especially one who was a friend of Miss Meecher. I recognized you the minute I saw your horse. You are the same man who stayed for a long visit several years back. Then when you left, I never saw Miss Meecher so . . . happy and sad all at the same time. Yes, I know you." The old man turned and led the way into the long, low, sod-roofed building.

Slocum slung the Appaloosa's reins around the hitching rail, ignored the horse's whicker of annoyance, and waited for the girl to precede him. She still glared at him, then turned, sweeping her skirts upward in a bold spin, and strode into the house before him. He couldn't help watching her as she headed in. And he had to admit, he had suddenly built up a hunger that he hoped would soon be satisfied, one way or another.

2

Slocum let his eyes adjust to the cooler, darker interior of the long, low front room of the roadhouse. He couldn't be sure, but he'd swear that much of the décor, if not all, was nearly the same as when he'd been through nearly three years before.

He'd been on a high-country manhunt back then, and had managed to track the bleeding fugitive to a cave where he'd holed up in the high rocks above Miss Meecher's place. Slocum and Marybeth had become acquainted then, both before and after he had managed to disarm and drag the outlaw down from the hills.

She had obligingly doctored the man's putrefying flesh wound. Later, Slocum had turned the man over to the nearest authority, a marshal down in Minton, and collected the bounty. Then he'd headed back north to Marybeth Meecher's roadhouse to try to repay her previous kindness in assisting with the fugitive.

He'd stayed on for a few months, gathering and chopping wood for the coming winter, repairing the ramshackle corral and sprung boards, and patching the leaking roofing on the house. All the while, she had made hospitality her number one priority. Rarely in his life had he ever been treated so well by a woman, nor so selflessly. Marybeth had wanted nothing from him, had seemed perfectly happy with him and with her lot in life.

She had an endearing, if a little worrisome, habit, as he recalled. She would drop whatever it was she was doing in order to help anyone who looked as though they required a leg up and over whatever it was they were struggling with. In his time there, she had boarded a couple of Crow Indian women from north of there who'd been abused somehow. And there had been that itinerant snake-oil salesman who had seemed entirely out of his element in the mountainous West. Slocum also remembered there being a quiet old Mexican man who lived in the barn and helped out with the place. Odd that he hadn't recognized the man right away.

The memory of those fine, if a bit odd, months brought a smile to his face. So where was Marybeth now? He tried not to think of dangerous possibilities just yet, but he did need answers from the old man.

As if reading his mind, the old man said, "What would you like to know, Mr. Slocum?" Miguel turned from sliding the big Dutch oven onto the scarred work surface of the long family-style table. Steam pulsed outward from beneath the rim of the black cast-iron top.

The question caught John Slocum by surprise. To his recollection, he hadn't told the man his name, but then again the old man seemed full of surprises. He apparently knew just who he was, remembered him, and seemed to enjoy this little game of amusement.

Play along, Slocum told himself, and you might eventually get answers. And a promising hot meal, which teased his twitching nostrils and slow, low-growling belly.

He plopped his hat upside down on an unused length of bench beside him and waited until the old man and girl were done bustling about the kitchen, ferrying a basket of what looked to be fresh-baked biscuits, a tub of butter, and a pot of coffee to the table. The girl laid out tin plates, silver spoons, folded cloth napkins, and china coffee cups.

"So you know my name. That means you have me, as they say, at a disadvantage."

"I am sorry, sir. But you are known to me." For the first

time the Mexican man smiled, a full, warm grin that lit his face. He extended a work-hardened hand toward the bench before Slocum. "Sit, sit, please, and I will explain everything." Then a sheepish look crossed his face. "If we do not, my hot-tempered granddaughter here just may toss the lot of it to the pig out back."

The girl flashed her sizzling eyes at the pair of them. "I would not, Grandfather, and you know it." She turned her withering gaze fully on Slocum. "I would dump it inside on a different pig."

The old man stood, the bench squawking backward along the smooth-worn floor beneath. "That is enough of this foolishness. While Miss Meecher is away, I am in charge here, and I tell you this is the way it will be. Now, no more games and silly wordplay. You will get along and you will enjoy this modest meal. Or at least you will keep quiet and pretend to enjoy yourself."

He knew the words were partially meant for him, so Slocum kept the grinning to a minimum, but he couldn't help stealing a peek at the chastened young woman. She sat at the far end of the table, closest to the stove and dry sink. He swore he saw steam rolling from the top of her pretty head, and he guessed that if she ground her teeth any tighter, they might powder.

The beans, as the prevailing aromas dictated, were a delectable if simple feast that he ate two helpings of, though only begrudgingly and at the insistence of the old man. It seemed to Slocum that they had less than most folks, and worked hard to maintain whatever reputation they might have left as a trailside eatery and a stop worthy of the name.

"Miss Meecher?" said Slocum between spoonfuls of beans and bites of biscuit sopping in bean juice.

"*Sí, sí.* Shortly after you were here nearly three years ago, my granddaughter came to live here. She had nowhere else to go. I was Miss Meecher's handyman and I was much needed, but Tita was most helpful, too. At that time, as you might recall, there were several stagecoaches through here a week, plus overlanders who are off the beaten trail and looking for respite before pressing onward west."

"Sounds like Marybeth got some much-needed help then."

"Yes, yes. She was a dear woman."

"Now there you go with that 'was' again." Slocum put down his coffee cup. "Is she . . . she's not dead, is she?"

The old man set down his own cup and rested his forehead in his hands. "I truthfully do not know, sir. I just do not know the answer to that." He looked up again. "She went away to help friends, and she has not come back since. That was three months ago?" He looked toward the girl for confirmation.

She nodded, looked sadly at her plate, and pushed beans around in their congealing juices, but did not eat.

"You see, as I mentioned, we were visited by some Indian friends. Crow, from the tribe across the border in Montana. It seems that members of their tribe were disappearing. They knew where, but their warriors were all dead or in white prisons. All that was left were old people like me, and mothers and their children."

"Where were they taken?" Slocum sipped his coffee. It was still hot enough to scald his tongue, so he blew across the surface.

The old man smiled again.

This is getting to be a habit, thought Slocum.

"The Triple T Ranch."

"And that's just where I was headed."

"I know, because you said you were going that way for work."

"How would you know?"

"I had a good idea," the old man tapped a gnarled finger to his temple.

"Oh, Grandpapa. You are silly now."

"Call me what you like, Granddaughter, but I know what I know. Am I wrong, Mr. Slocum?"

"No, no, you're not. But enough of the suspense. If there's something I should know about Indians disappearing, and Marybeth Meecher disappearing, and Lord knows what else, please tell me."

"In truth, Mr. Slocum, I don't know all that much about it for certain, but I will tell you what I think I know. I think that the ranch where you hope to find employment is not much of a ranch anymore."

"What do you mean?"

The girl groaned and let her spoon clatter to her plate, her untouched beans glazing over as they cooled. "Don't tell me you are that stupid, Mr. Slocum?"

"Tita!"

"No, Grandpapa. I can tell that this one is bad. He is going to go up there and tell them all he knows and then soon we, too, will be dragged away in the night and put to work in that slave camp."

Slocum stood up fast enough that the bench he sat on stuttered on the wood floor, then toppled backward. He didn't care, except that he saw it pinched his hat. He balled up his napkin and tossed it on the table. "All right, what's this about a slave camp? One of you had better give me a straight answer or I'm liable to—"

"What?" she said, standing also. "What is it you will do, Mr. Slocum? Since you are a guest in this house and we have done nothing to harm you, I would like to know what a big, angry man like you will do."

He pointed a finger at her. "I'll think of something. But if I can't get a straight answer out of you, and there are people whose lives are in danger, and one of them is Marybeth Meecher, I can only assume that you both are happy to know that she's gone."

The old man gasped and the girl for the first time lost her scowl. The old man stood up. "How dare you say such a thing and in our . . . that is to say, this house."

Slocum bent and straightened the bench. "About time I got a rise out of you. Now if you truly don't tell me what I need to know, then we're done here and I'm going to go off and find out for myself. And if I find that you've been playing Marybeth false, then I promise I will cause you both no end of trouble, mark my words."

The room was silent. The woman and her grandfather both sat looking down at their plates like scolded children. Slocum felt badly about his outburst, even knowing that his frustration with the pair of them was justified. They talked in circles, hinting at something nefarious but either not knowing enough to substantiate such claims or, worse, knowing more than they let on and teasing and taunting him with the information.

"Grandfather is right," said the girl, meeting his gaze. "We do not know much more than we have said, but we have strong suspicions that the Triple T Ranch to which you ride is run by a greedy man who has made much in the way of riches, but very little of it with cattle."

"Then what is he getting rich from? I was led to believe by a friend back in Dodge that it was a working cattle ranch. One of the biggest in Montana, he told me."

"Ah, it used to be." The old man smiled. "I remember those days. For years, there was more work than the owners could hire for. And so the men who did work there were well paid and well fed and given good mounts. This was not that long ago."

"What happened?"

"The ranch was sold."

"It was stolen!" said the girl. "Stolen by that foul man Colonel Mulletson."

"That's the man whose name I was given," said Slocum.

The old man nodded. "Yes, yes, he is the owner of the Triple T now. But it was not always the case. Since he took over, and brought his own men in, letting go good local wranglers and cowboys and stockmen, the ranch and its lands have become less and less used as the years have gone by."

The old man shook his head. When he raised it, his eyes were glistening. "Now the few cattle that are there are weak and diseased, ranging free and slowly getting picked off by the weather and bandits. At least the Crow are getting some use out of them, but that's the only good thing."

"I just don't understand what could possess a man to buy— or however he got the place—such a vast and valuable ranch, then let it go downhill like he has. And you say he still makes money?"

"Not just money, Mr. Slocum," said the girl, clearing the table. "But more money than you have ever seen."

"Doing what?"

"Gold, of course," said the old man. He spread his hands wide in explanation. "At least that is what we are told by the Indians. But they have been so driven apart by the white men—I mean no offense—that they are powerless to do much about it. And any complaints they make to the law have fallen on deaf ears."

"So he's using the people who have disappeared as labor? Are they at least being paid?"

"I don't think they're being paid at all, Mr. Slocum. Many go in and few ever are seen again."

"You can't mean . . . but that's slavery." Slocum scratched his stubbled chin and walked to the dead fireplace. "Slave labor in a gold mine?"

"Yes, that is what I suspect."

"What makes you think it's a gold mine?"

"I have no proof, of course," said the old man, his hands held up, shoulders hunched. "But . . ."

The girl went back to the stove, slammed the lid back down on the firebox, and tuned to face Slocum. "I know this for certain. I have the proof. I have seen it with my own two eyes."

"Tita! I thought we agreed, never again!" The old man's eyes were wide.

"I was there again! I rode out one night not long after Miss Meecher was taken away."

"Yes, yes, I know about that time."

"But I went again a month ago."

"But you did not tell me of this!" The old man slapped a hand flat on the tabletop. He was more animated than Slocum had seen him since they'd nearly traded gunshots earlier.

Slocum held up his hand and shook his head. "I don't mean to interrupt this touching family moment, but I need to know what you saw, Tita."

"Why? Do you really think you are going to do something about it? Do you think we are so stupid to believe you won't just ride out of here and never look back?" She snorted, shook her head. "Ha, you will just turn us over to those pigs. I bet there's good money in slaves, eh?"

Slocum ground his teeth together, and chose not to respond

to the rude young woman. The entire episode felt like a huge waste of his time and he wished he could have skipped stopping here. But the promise of seeing Marybeth again had been too much.

Now that he had stopped, he had to know what had happened to Marybeth. If she had gone up there on her own, looking to help her friends, she probably ended up a slave herself. Or worse.

3

There was only one thing Slocum had wanted more than sleep that night, and that thing seemed entirely impossible now. The sultry Mexican girl, given her raised-lip demeanor, and her glaring ways, wanted nothing to do with him. He got the impression, from the first moments of their meeting, that she would like nothing more than to gut him with a dull spoon. So, he told himself, sleep is what you'll have to be satisfied with, Slocum.

And sleep is what he accepted as good enough for that night—the tail end of a very long day in the saddle. His thoughts drifted briefly to his horse, the Appaloosa, in the same stable, two stalls over. He imagined the big, muscled beast was feeling much the same way. The horse surely knew that tomorrow would bring more of the same, so no doubt, unlike dumb humans, he had long since worked his way through his bate of hay and had drifted into a long restorative slumber.

Slocum's eyelids pulled downward, felt leaden with the weight of the day. His years-long habit of checking the shadows, probing with his mind the last of the day's half-lit corners, lost the battle to keep his eyes open and his mind awake.

But the honed mind of a wanted man is never fully at rest, and Slocum's last thought, as it had been on many of his nights on the vast, green earth, were of his plight as a roving soul.

He was wanted for a crime for which he was innocent. The killing of that corrupt judge was a long time in the past, but it was still a millstone around his neck. The memory of it plagued him at least once a day, and usually at night, just as his mind wound down, finally at ease after another in an endless string of long days.

But on this night, John Slocum's razor-stropped senses, even in the final clutches of a fast-approaching and deep slumber, detected the faintest rustling of soft dry dirt underfoot. Not under a boot, though, softer and more muffled, as if under a bare foot.

In the time it takes for a fly to change course or a thought to pass from curiosity to conviction, John Slocum's mind turned on a dime. In that same instant his mind burst wide and fully awake, his Colt Navies palmed and cocked. His wire-taut body, tenser than spring steel, had whipped upright, his wool blanket dropping to his midsection. His bare chest expanded and lessened ever so faintly in the faintest glow of moonlight from the half-open stable door.

A form had passed through the cracked door, of that he was sure, though he did not witness it. The air in the barn had somehow changed. It was a stinging thing pulsing with a bitter, palpable taste. His first instinct was to whisper, "Who's there?"

But his drifter's curiosity overrode that silly instinct. He would wait them out. Somehow he knew it was a human, and not a prowling cougar or starved coyote. It was a human, and whoever it was wanted something bad enough to slink in the shadows.

"Slocum? John Slocum?"

It was the Mexican girl. He'd know that voice in a town of hundreds. Mostly because it seemed, for reasons unknown to him, every word she had said all night had been spoken in anger. Why is that, Slocum? he thought. What had he done to this foul-intentioned woman to provoke such hissing and sparking and clawing?

"Here," he said, but he did not like the way his voice sounded. It was hoarse, trembly, and weak.

And then she appeared before him, skylined in the faint

moonglow from the partially opened barn door. "I was hoping you would be awake."

"Why?" he said before he remembered he'd vowed to keep his mouth shut around her.

"Because, you . . . you disgust me." She moved closer. He could see her fully now, wearing what looked like a shapeless nightgown, but the moonglow behind her outlined her astounding shape. Hers was a working woman's body, thin, lithe, muscular, bold, and strong. She wore nothing that he could see beneath the thin cotton gown.

"You . . . you make me want to handle a gun. But that is something my grandfather has forbidden me. All because I am a woman. He seems to think that because I am female, he must protect me. Who does he think took care of me for the two years before he found me? I was alone on the streets of Tijuana, begging for scraps, licking the plates of the wealthy before their kitchen staff could see me when I wriggled through the windows. For such, I owe him my life, but . . ."

As he listened, Slocum, pistol still drawn, considered his next move and decided it would be based on hers. He didn't have long to wait.

She strode to him purposefully, on bare feet, and slammed her belly into his. "You disgust me, John Slocum," she hissed. She ground her waist and her hips into his, her tongue flicking like a serpent's.

Slocum's eased off his pistols' triggers, too surprised by the moment to holster them.

"For an angry woman, and someone who really seems to dislike me, you sure have an odd way of showing it."

"Shut up and kiss me before I find something else to hate about you."

Slocum holstered his pistols, and unable to resist her hateful advances, he gripped her backside through the gauzy flannel. "I think I can find something that might please you."

And he matched her tongue's ardent ministrations with his own, all the while thinking that he seriously doubted anything would put a smile on this little hellcat's face. At that moment, he didn't really care if she was smiling or not. Just that she kept on doing what she was doing.

Before he knew what had happened, she had wriggled out of the thin nightgown, her kissing barely pausing even when the nightgown passed up and over her face.

"I doubt that, gringo . . . and I am willing to try to prove you wrong."

The heat rising from her taut body, like a flat rock in the desert at midday, warmed his muscled belly. Her lips trailed down his ridged chest, pausing to tease and flick at his nipples, and his breath caught in his throat. This was not something he'd expected from this woman, this bold, seemingly spiteful woman. But there would be ample time for pondering over the whys behind this . . . later. Right now, he found it quite simple enough to concentrate on the task she seemed intent on performing.

As she licked and teased her way down the long, muscled plane of his chest and stomach, her nimble fingers, as hot to the touch as was her searching, busy mouth, all but ripped off his gun belt and denims. She slid his trousers down over his backside and he heard her utter a soft grunt of surprise and satisfaction as she bumped her face against his lust-thickened member.

Slocum's hands found their way blind and groping, his fingers tangling in her thick, dark hair. But she needed no urging, for she trailed her tongue up from the thatch of hair at its root, sliding her hot tongue up its long, stiff length, not neglecting a spot as she laved him, grunting and making small, hoarse sounds deep in the back of her throat.

When her mouth reached the pulsing tip, pearling with anticipation, she teased, with her perfect white teeth, dragging them forward along the sensitive head.

Even in the near dark, he knew she was enjoying this torture she was putting him through. He felt her strong hands on either side of his buttocks, and without warning, she pulled him hard toward her, driving her face forward once, twice, three times, descending the full length of his shaft before gently raking him with her teeth back to the tip. She never quite let go nor broke the pressure with her lips, hot and formed to him as if made for the task.

All too soon he had to force her back from him, knowing what would happen if she had her full way down there. He would be spent and unable to indulge himself in other ways, nor please her as much as she was doing for him. As he eased her mouth from him, she uttered a small growl of what he suspected, coming from her, to be anger.

He pulled her to her feet and rolled her nipples until they jutted like underripe raspberries. She gasped and bit into his shoulder with each tender squeeze he gave. She slid one leg up and down his, teasingly close. With each pass, he could feel her heat as he kissed then sucked at her breasts.

The girl began trembling then and reached down between his legs, her breath stuttering as if she'd run a great distance. She was ready for him and he slid into her as if it was the one task he had always been meant to do. She exhaled, a long, tremulous sound, and a breeze flickered the gauzy cobwebs in the bare window. Far off in the night, a coyote yipped his long, plaintive sound.

Slocum eased out, and the girl's inner muscles kneaded his member as it slid, as if begging him to reconsider. And he did, for just as quickly he plunged in again, deeper and quicker this time, and the girl's breathing mimicked the action. In and out he drove with increasing rapidity until there was no way she could keep up, and her hips bucked and swayed with the man's hard-driving power.

Just when Slocum thought he was nearly finished, the girl had a peculiar way of slowing the motion, of easing him back from the brink, all without touching him with her hands.

"What are you doing to me?" he said, half kidding, and half exhausted, but not wanting it to end just yet. He had a hunch she wasn't through.

"Shut up. Do not talk to me—I am still not sure I trust you."

"And this is the way you judge such things?"

Her response was to grip him harder down there, nearly pinching off his breathing before plunging him deep inside her once again. The result made them both exhale, then they were off to the races again, both plunging and bucking wildly. He spun her over so that she was on her back and he took full and final command of the situation, making her bite down on the cloth of her wadded-up dress and howl into it, lest her grandfather hear their heated, animal sounds.

Just as they finished, each locked in a trembling last spasm, she did a curious thing—she gripped him even tighter and wrapped her legs around his back. For a moment she hugged him as if her life depended on it. And then she let go.

In a moment, she had rolled over, her back tight to his front. They fit together like two spoons, and holding his arm across her belly, she fell asleep. Slocum lay awake a long time, thinking of the strange turn of events the day had taken, of the woman he was now with.

She meant little more to him than he did to her—they were both there to satisfy a mutual instant need for companionship, nothing more. Unlike the woman who owned this place, Marybeth Meecher, this girl was to him like the flare of a match instead of the bone-soaking heat of a winter fire.

Where was Marybeth now? Why hadn't she come back home to her beloved roadhouse? She was a determined woman with nothing but the kindness of others behind all her actions. So it didn't surprise him that she would have lit out for parts unknown in search of stray souls in need of help.

But the fact that she hadn't returned did trouble Slocum greatly. Marybeth was a resourceful woman, yes, but not the type to go off on a fool's errand without adequate planning. Had the old man and his granddaughter told him the truth? Had they done something to her and taken over her establishment for themselves?

The old man seemed to know Marybeth and seemed genuinely fond of her, and Slocum had remembered him from his time here three years before. Then, though, the man had seemed guarded and wary of nearly everyone. But that was the way often with people who had little themselves and who were trying to maintain a tenuous connection to something, anything that they felt would ensure them some form of security in life.

Surely Slocum had lived much of his life that way, too. He couldn't fault the old man for that. And he did seem like a decent sort. Not lying, just adequately guarded. And then once he had realized Slocum was willing to help, it seemed to open up a whole new level of trust within the old man.

But the girl, she was a conundrum. Full of spite and anger, hate even. That she cared for her grandfather was evident, though not in any traditional sense. She seemed a damaged soul, one who had perhaps been through much that others might never know about—at least not from her. But beyond that, Slocum wasn't sure about her except that she seemed to be hiding something.

And in the morning, vowed Slocum, he'd find out just what it was. He bet it had something to do with the whereabouts of Marybeth Meecher.

4

It was a boot on gravel that woke Slocum. He sat up, heard another boot step, then two more right after. That meant two people, probably men, and one of them wasn't the old Mexican, who would be barefoot.

He felt the girl tense beside him. "Grandfather!" she hissed, struggling to her feet. He held on to her and she thrashed at his grip.

"Stay here, dammit," he whispered. "We don't know who they are, but if what you told me is true, they're probably looking for you and him. I can help him better if I'm not worrying about you, too."

"Then you'll just have to worry." And with that, she was gone, hadn't even bothered to pull on her nightgown.

He tugged on his second boot and strapped on his gun belt, then he, too, slipped through the door. How had anyone ridden in here without him hearing? He cursed himself, but he knew why—she had worked him hard, riding him like someone who wants to win a race at all costs, no matter the health of the mount.

He had to put the girl out of his mind for now. She was a tough number and too headstrong for her own good, but she was on her own at least for the next few minutes.

"We seen a girl!"

Groans rose into the otherwise still, chill night air.

"I said we seen a girl! Now where is she?"

"No, no, there is no girl here. You are mistaken, sir. It is only me. I'm here alone. An old man with no—"

More sounds of hard beatings followed, then silence.

"Rollins, dammit. I think you killed him." One of the men toed the still form on the floor before them. He flopped, lay still. "Yep, I'd say so. You killed a perfectly good slave, you dumb bastard. Boss ain't gonna like this. He will have our hide for this, sure as Sundays are for prayin'."

"Nah, he's just knocked out."

Then another voice mumbled something, too low for Slocum to hear. He eased out the barn door and bolted in a low run through the inky night, the cool mountain air chilling his bare chest and arms. He ran as fast as he could across the yard, a pistol drawn, a grim set to his mouth. Save the old man and the girl; that was all he had room for in his mind. But damn, he'd have been happier if she'd stayed put.

"And a girl. We seen a man and a girl. You hear me, you bean eater?" Something stiff and hard rammed into something softer with a thud, raising a gasp and more groans.

Someone's getting a mighty beating, thought Slocum as he eased the trigger back on his pistol and cat-footed around the barn, the girl's scent still on the air before him.

Slocum felt his way around the far end of the house, vaguely recalling that there was a long, low wooden box, painted red, that Marybeth had used to store firewood, extra Dutch ovens, all manner of gear. His knee struck it sooner than he'd expected and it was all he could do to keep from crying out.

"Rupe, you hear that?"

"What?"

"From outside, out back yonder. Some sort of noise."

"Well, check on it, numb nuts. I got to do everything here?"

Their voices slumped down to a whisper, still loud enough for Slocum to hear.

"All right, all right. Keep your clothes on. First thing's first. I'm going to finish off this here Mexican while you go— Well! What have we here? Hey, Rollins, we got ourselves a pretty little chica—and nekkid as the day is long, too!"

Slocum heard raw, braying laughter along with the continued groans of the old man.

"You leave my grandfather alone. Now!" The girl spat the words at them. Slocum had to give it to her—she was a handful of hot coals.

He stepped once, twice more then drove a boot hard against the wood-and-twine lift-latch. Planks cracked and split lengthwise and Slocum slammed his way through, the door swinging inward, rattling hard against a sideboard. He heard something topple, fall to the wood floor. Dim light from a low-burning oil lamp wavered with the gust of fresh air.

"What the—" The man speaking spun toward the door. He was a broad-shouldered fat man with a massive shaggy heard and a too-small shapeless felt hat stuck on top. He reminded Slocum of a man with a bull bison's head attached. The man had a repeating rifle poised at waist height, but he never got the chance to pull the trigger intentionally.

Slocum sent two rounds straight into the man, one in the center of his massive coat-covered chest, just under the shaggy beard. The other a little higher. It split the bridge of the brute's nose and punched straight into his brain. But the man kept on coming.

Slocum had enough time to see the naked girl launch herself at the turned back of the other man, a thinner fellow, just as tall, and with a lean, muscled look about him. She'd screamed and locked her wildcat arms about the man's neck. He turned from Slocum, the girl's naked body swinging behind him like an angry living garment. Her flailing legs and bucking body did their best to keep from his swatting grasp and inflict some sort of pain at the same time. Slocum saw that the brute would slam the girl into a wall or the mantel any second, and no matter how game she was, a few hard slams and she'd crumple.

Slocum cranked three more rounds into the advancing bison man and with the last was relieved to see the big beast stop short, lurch as if pushed from behind. He dropped the rifle and a great rush of air and blood geysered upward from his mouth. He dove forward like a great falling redwood.

Slocum didn't wait to see the man drop, but drove himself

at the dervishing pair of combatants. True to Slocum's suspicions, the man began to work backward toward the fireplace mantel even while it looked to Slocum as if the girl was biting his ear. She tightened her grip on his neck, doing her damnedest to choke the fiend.

The mantel was just the height he'd need to disrupt her once and for all. But Slocum intervened just before they staggered into the projecting hewn shelf. He wished the girl would just drop off so he could deal with the man. He wanted him alive so he might force information out of him. He had a strong suspicion these two were out on a gathering mission for the slavery outfit.

He found his opening, and grabbing the man by the shirtfront, he was able to slam him in the temple with the butt of his Colt. The man stopped growling and swatting at the girl on his back and stared at Slocum with a look of glazing surprise. One nostril fluttered, working like a bellows with his ragged breathing.

He looked like he was chewing on something and then gagging as he wavered in Slocum's grasp.

"Gaah . . ."

Slocum realized it was probably the girl's fingers, but she didn't utter a scream, just a long string of Mexican lingo, half of which Slocum could pick out, the other half whipped by too fast for him to comprehend. But the meaning was clear: This woman was still very much brimming with anger.

Just before the man dropped to the floor, the girl, lithe as a cougar in the high rocks, leapt from the man's back, and stood to the side, one hand shaking off the chewing the man had given her fingers, the other already reaching for the cooled-off frying pan. She brought it up high. It clunked off a beam, then Slocum stiff-armed her and snatched the pan from her grasp.

"You bastardo! You dare! He hurt my grandfather!" And with that reminder, she ran to the old man. Miguel, Slocum saw, hadn't moved, and a spreading pool of blood beneath his head foretold the worst.

He moved to the old man, bent low over him, but the girl's sagged features and silent tears told him even before he verified for himself that the man's heart had stopped. They had beaten him to death, and he and the girl had been in the barn not far away. Why in God's name hadn't he heard them?

He walked to the door and leaned into the battered frame. Nothing moved outside. It would be light in another hour or so. With any luck he would be able to get some sort of information out of the man he'd coldcocked.

As he turned back to the room, he saw girl looking across the room toward the prone man, saw the same man, pistol drawn, temple bloodied, thumbing back the hammer. The son of a bitch was aiming to shoot an unarmed naked girl. And she didn't seem afraid in the least. Just angry.

"Get down!" Slocum shouted and dropped to one knee. All in one smooth, oft-repeated motion, once more he clawed free his Colt, palmed it, peeled back the hammer, and squeezed the trigger. The bullet caught the prone man in the neck. A gagging sound bubbled out of him, his eyes rolled back, then his forehead hit the floor with a thunk. Only then did his pistol drop.

As life slipped from the man, his finger convulsed, tightened on the trigger. The bullet caromed into the stone fireplace, spanged off blackened rock within, and whizzed like a bee past Slocum's head before lodging in a corner beam.

By the time dawn broke, the girl had prepared her grandfather's body for burial. Slocum had regretted killing the two men, though only because they possessed information he would need. Now his trip north to the Triple T was more a mission than a journey for a job. Bad things were happening there, and the emissaries of that place had nearly gotten him killed. Worse, they had killed a decent old man looking for nothing more than to provide for his only relative left alive, his granddaughter.

And now she was angrier than before—and alone in the world. He toed the last of the two killers into the hole he'd dug for them, beyond a low rise well away from the buildings.

By the time he came back to the kitchen, the girl had a pot of coffee on the stove to boil, and had cleaned herself up at the trough where Slocum had first encountered the old man.

"I would like your help with the winding sheet, and then we can bury him. I will dig the hole."

"No, I will dig the hole. Just tell me where. It's the least I can do for him." Slocum stared at the dead man. She'd done an admirable job. He looked peaceful and kind, almost as he had when he'd offered Slocum a rare smile at dinner the night before.

Slocum looked at the girl. To his surprise, she looked calm and simply nodded. "Okay then. Follow me. But have a cup of coffee first." She poured him one, then one for herself. They sipped them in silence.

When they were done, she set the tin cups in the dry sink and walked outdoors. He retrieved the shovel from where he'd leaned it earlier by the door, and followed her to a slight rise just to the east of the house. Short, scrubby pines wreathed the spot. From it, the view of the surrounding landscape was serene and restful.

As if reading his thoughts, the girl said, "Grandfather liked to sit here. He even cleared it of sage so his chair fit the ground better." One side of her mouth rose and she almost smiled. Then it faded. "So here is where he shall be buried. I will dig first." She looked at Slocum. "I must help with some of it."

It was a simple statement that he understood held a deeper meaning. It would be important for her to share in this final task of burying her grandfather. He nodded and handed her the shovel.

5

Several hours later, with aching muscles and an empty belly, Slocum thought of "slaves" and "Boss," words that echoed in his mind from the talk of the men he'd killed. Slocum stood holding the Appaloosa's reins in one hand, the reins of a well-tended chestnut mare in the other. He'd taken the liberty of saddling it for Tita.

"What are you doing?" she said, eyeing the second horse.

"You're going with me. You won't be safe here alone. I think we've discovered that much. There's to be no arguments, no more of this scowling, angry person you seem to enjoy playing at."

She stood in the doorway of the little roadhouse. The door, repaired to the best of Slocum's ability, moved in an unfelt breeze, a faint squeak the only sound. The distress and lack of sleep of the night before had taken their toll on the girl's still unblemished features.

Dark smudges had blossomed beneath her coffee-colored eyes, and her scowl had lessened in intensity, now replaced with something more akin to a weariness that Slocum suspected would be there for some time to come. The girl, it seemed, had not had an easy row to hoe in her young life. And recent events didn't promise anything easier for some time to come.

"Okay, John Slocum. But I warn you—I do what I want, I take what I want, and I give what I want. I think I have made that plain."

He nodded, touched his hat brim. "Yes, ma'am. I don't know what we're headed for, and I can't promise you'll be back this way, so I'd suggest gathering what you might regret not having with you, then we best get riding."

She pulled in a long, deep breath, let it out, and turned back to the dark of the cabin. Slocum barely had time to mount up before she came back out, closed the door behind her, and tossed a gunny sack of supplies to him. He peeked in the floppy top, saw a slab of bacon, a sack of coffee, another of beans, a few knobs of hard tack, and what looked like a small amount of cornmeal. He nodded, cinched the top tight, and looped it over the saddle horn.

The girl mounted the chestnut mare, another sack with what he guessed were items of clothing tied bandolier style across her chest. Her grandfather's shotgun she stuffed into the empty boot beside the saddle.

"That everything you're taking along?"

"All I really need is in my head." She tapped her temple in much the same fashion as her grandfather did the night before. On him the mannerism had carried with it a slight amusement; on her it bore a sober weight of import.

Slocum nodded once and clucked to the Appaloosa. He tapped his heels to the big horse's belly and headed back to the road.

He looked back once, checked to see that she was trailing behind, and she caught his eye. Without a word, she urged her mount forward and rode abreast of him, saying nothing. They rode that way for some time, Slocum enjoying the sun on his face, and the open spaces affording him a chance to clear his mind and put some thought into just what it was he was riding into.

At the top of a long rise in the rough, wheel-gouged road, they let the horses blow and climbed down, stretching their backs and rubbing their backsides.

"From what I've been told, we should be there tomorrow at this time. But since we're getting close, I don't want to draw any more attention to us than we need to. What's say we head over there, just to the west, pick our way through those hills. We'll be higher up than this roadway and we can see what's what from there."

The girl regarded him a moment. "You sound as if you sense trouble heading our way."

He shrugged. "When isn't it? I've found that if you stay still long enough, trouble finds you eventually. Why risk it?"

The girl almost smiled, then seemed to remember who she was, nodded once, and mounted up. He followed suit and they headed up into the sparsely treed hills that grew thicker with vegetation the higher up they climbed. Less than an hour had passed before Slocum held a hand low, waist height, and motioned for her to stop.

"Riders ahead. Coming this way," he said, not turning. "Dismount, lead 'em slow so we don't kick up dust." He looked to their left. "There, up behind that tumbledown. We'll wait them out."

When they were concealed, he slipped a brass telescope from his saddlebag and extended it.

The girl touched his sleeve. "The reflection—won't they see it?"

"Shouldn't, the sun's behind us."

He pinched one eye shut and rotated the device until the travelers came into focus. "Two men on lathered horses, riding at a steady clip. Not showing any sign they see us."

He handed the telescope to the girl. She mimicked his eye squint and focusing motions. He watched her face, then saw by the stiffening in her neck that she'd spotted them, too.

"They have the look of the two from last night."

"Yep," he said, taking the telescope. "I reckon they're from the same outfit. Probably out here on the same patrol, maybe headed this way expecting to meet up with the others." He focused in on them again. "They don't look like happy people, do they?"

"Sometimes you say strange things, John Slocum."

He looked at her but she wasn't smiling. He shook his head. What could a man say to that?

All went well until the riding men were nearly abreast of

them on the roadside below. Slocum's horse nickered and the chestnut followed suit. The riding men slowed and Slocum noted that they were savvy enough to pay attention to their mounts. And that meant that they'd probably start looking around them, cautious, as men engaged in questionable acts usually are.

The men reined up, looking from their mounts' perked ears toward the hillside to the west. Slocum and the girl crouched low, each keeping a hand on their horse's muzzle to quiet them. It was times like this that Slocum resented the social instincts of horses. More than once a friendly or curious whicker from the Appaloosa had landed him in hot water.

The two riders still hadn't seen them, and though it was Slocum's preference not to hide in the rocks but to stand and deliver, he also had the girl to think of. Despite not quite knowing what to do with her, it was quickly proving to have been a mistake to bring her along. Too late now, he told himself.

And then the men both seemed to swivel their heads right toward them. What had given them away? He'd thought they were pretty well hidden. Then he saw that he'd been watching them too intently to notice that the girl had risen up a bit and was in the process of shucking her shotgun from her saddle's boot.

They must have seen her. He didn't know what part of her they'd spied, but it didn't matter. He reached out and slapped at the closest thing he could to get her attention—her backside. His eyes said it all. She dropped down low, cradling the shotgun and wincing with unspoken apology, but as she watched the men, she realized it was too late.

They were peeling apart, each picking a fast path up into the rocky, rolling slope not far below them, but sticking to cover. It was what he'd do—bookend them, but stay hidden, as they were doing. Slocum nodded as he kept low, shucked his rifle. He wanted to get a clear shot at them, but as of yet, they hadn't proved themselves to be worthy of dying, though he knew that was just a formality. He could feel their hydrophobic-dog ways, knew they were hungry killers.

"You . . . up there in the rocks! We seen you!"

Slocum racked in a round, let the sound carry, and said, "Back out of here. Leave me be. I'm a broke-down prospector—I ain't done a thing to you all!"

"Ha! Then you're the prettiest prospector I ever did see, mister. I don't know who you are, but I bet I know who she is. Come on down here, baby!"

Slocum heard the twin hammers peeling back before he turned. He knew what he'd see, and he wasn't wrong.

There stood the girl, just behind him, a genuine smile on her face. "I said I take what I want, didn't I?"

Slocum tried to ease himself around to face her, but she shook her head. "I don't think so, John Slocum. That rifle stays pointed right where it is. You wait until the boys get up here."

"They your boys?"

"Sometimes yes, sometimes no."

"Let me guess, the boys from last night—yours, too?"

She shrugged.

"Were you broken up about them or about your grandfather?"

Her face chilled again and her eyes narrowed. "You shut up about Grandfather. That was never supposed to happen."

"Then why all this?"

She eyed him but didn't answer. Heavy, clumsy boot steps scraping gravel drew closer behind him.

"Welcome to the party, boys," said Slocum. "I guess you were expecting us."

After a few seconds, a shadow darkened just behind him. Slocum looked up to see a broad man blotting out a lot of blue sky. That would be the first one of the two he'd seen through the telescope.

The man stared down at him for a few seconds, then said, "Tita, this man . . . he do any hurtin' to you at all?"

The girl snorted, stifling a laugh, and shook her head. "No, no, Gabe. I am still your pure-as-snow angel."

They heard the second man before they saw him. He came slowly up from the south, kicking rocks and cursing between hard-won breaths. By the time he staggered into view, Slocum saw why the man spent most of his time wheezing—he had the blue-veined face of a hardcore drinker, and though he could barely stand, he was about to light a fresh-rolled quirly from the remnants of the smoking tag end of the one between his blue lips.

"Have a nice walk?" Slocum knew he shouldn't have said anything, but the man was a sore sight. You keep up with the wise answers, he told himself, and you'll never get off this slope alive.

The man's hand hovered over his holstered pistol. But the trigger was still laced down.

Gabe, the big boy, said, "Shut it, mister. We'd as soon have you alive, but it won't make much never mind if you're chewing dirt. Your call."

Slocum shifted his glance to the girl, who seemed amused by the entire affair.

"Honey," said Slocum to the girl. "You don't really expect me to believe you'd take up with a grunter like this guy, do you? Especially not after last night."

For two full seconds nothing happened. Then everything did. Slocum winked at the girl and rolled onto his left shoulder just as the big Gabe stomped forward, placing himself smack between Slocum and the girl.

As he rolled, Slocum slicked a Colt from its holster and peeled back the hammer. He was faster than both Gabe and the girl, who had stepped forward to get a shot around the big man.

Slocum's first shot cored the brute's shoulder and jerked him backward into the girl's shotgun. She lurched away, yanking the triggers as she misstepped. Gabe took the full brunt low in the back.

Meanwhile the smoker had grabbed enough air to yell a garble of words that Slocum was sure weren't very nice. As soon as he freed that knotted rawhide, he yanked on his pistol and Slocum's Colt barked once, followed by the rifle. One of the shots drove just above the hat line on the man's forehead, exposed when he'd pushed back his hat after his long walk up the hill.

His ears ringing and his right foot wedged under the

flopped deadweight of Gabe, Slocum holstered his pistol and kept his rifle leveled on the girl. The shotgun was unloaded, but he wasn't taking any chances. She was a lithe little thing; maybe she'd make a play for Gabe's dropped piece. Slocum couldn't see where it had ended up.

It had all happened so fast that he wasn't sure if she understood just what occurred. And then she screamed.

This much emotion from the girl shocked Slocum, but not enough to slow him down from freeing his foot. By the time he was upright, she had stopped and looked at him with that same old anger, boiling and snapping in her eyes like far-horizon heat lightning on a still summer night.

He stepped wide around Gabe. Three triggers' worth into him meant he was most likely dead, but he'd seen his share of dead men rise up and kill. A rifle length from the girl, Slocum reached with his pistol hand and grabbed the warm barrel ends of the shotgun, twisted it out of her grasp. She staggered backward one, two steps, then crossed her arms and stared at him. The shotgun and her shirt and skirt fronts were flecked with blood spatter, but other than that, she seemed much as she had the evening before.

"Killing isn't easy," he said. "Especially if it's a friend. But you offered me no choice."

She turned from him, made to mount up, but he shook his head. "No, no I don't think so, little sister. You just stay right there, hands on the saddle just like that."

He walked over to her, retrieved a length of hemp rope from his saddlebag. "I normally use this bit of rope to tie the legs of game before I hoist them up into trees for butchering. But I figure you'll naturally want to make a break for it, try to outfox me, maybe even shoot me." He leaned close to her ear and, in a low voice, said, "Despite what we meant to each other just last night."

Her response came out in a low, throaty growl. How much anger could one person hold? He shook his head and gave the rope another hard tug before securing it around her wrists in front of her.

Once he satisfied himself that she was of little threat, bound and unable to mount up on the chestnut without his assistance, Slocum busied himself with rummaging through the dead men's pockets. He took shells off the men, since they would fit his rifle, but left the rest. Least he could do, he figured. It was grim work, as death always is, and he was relieved that she hadn't chosen that moment to become chatty. Killing sometimes did that to a person. There'd be plenty of time to press her for information while they were on the trail.

He wasn't quite sure he knew what he was going to do with her or if he should even continue on to the ranch. Maybe he should head back to Minton, turn her over to his old acquaintance, Marshal Owens. Tell the marshal what he knew about the supposed slave operation, then head back up to the Triple T and try to find Marybeth. Dammit, but he'd been looking forward to a decent-paying ranch job without complications.

"Problems, John Slocum?"

"Yeah, you could say that. And you appear to be the biggest of them all."

She smiled and shook her head. "You know you are making a big mistake."

"Oh?" He let the wheezing man's corpse drop beside his fat friend, Gabe, then straightened and rubbed his back. "How's that?"

"Yes, you see, I was playing those men like a violin. They were supposed to get me information, lead me to the bastard at the heart of the slavery, the man behind it all."

"And that would be?"

"Colonel Mulletson, of course."

"So, you have been there at least once before, right? Don't suppose you'd care to tell me about the place? What I might expect when I get there?"

He stood beside her, held his fingers laced together for her to step into. She swung her leg up and surprised him by not trying to kick him in the chin as she settled into the saddle. She wore the split skirt preferred by most women serious about riding.

"What about them? And their horses?"

"We'll leave the bodies here, no time for buryin'. And we'll check the horses on our way downslope, see what their saddlebags have to offer."

But it turned out that the men's bags held nothing of value and what foodstuffs were there—flour, coffee—were scant and not worth their time. Slocum fashioned a lead line for each of the men's horses and trailed them behind their own mounts.

"What will you tell them at the ranch?"

"About what?" said Slocum.

She sighed. Good, he thought. Means she's growing as tired of this ruse as I am.

"You will show up with the horses of two dead men, with me tied up like a . . . a pig! And no bodies of the dead men. What will you tell them?"

"I'm sure something will come to me. Right now, we need to make tracks." He had a feeling if he held his peace, then the girl would get antsy and tell him what she should have told him the day before.

She held out longer than he would have guessed, but then again, nothing about this girl shocked him anymore. It was nearly two hours later that her voice, cracking from lack of water, breached the silence of travel across long, dry passages.

"Slocum, I need to get down for a minute and I need water."

"Maybe later. Right now we have too much ground to cover."

Another few minutes passed, then she said, "Look, I am not who you think I am. I am . . . more like the girl you saw before, last night, all right?"

He turned in the saddle and regarded her. "That doesn't help one bit. You are who you are? What am I supposed to do with that?"

"I am telling you, if we just ride into the ranch like we are now . . ."

"What will happen?"

"I don't really know."

They both fell silent again for a minute, each watching far-off clouds scud low across the horizon.

"I only went there because my grandfather was so worried

about Miss Meecher. She meant everything to him, and when she didn't come back, he was very upset."

"I can understand. Miss Meecher had that effect on other folks."

"You, too?"

He didn't answer, but urged his horse forward.

"You're a tough man, aren't you, John Slocum?"

Again, he said nothing for a while. "What did you find out at the ranch?"

"That Miss Meecher is there. Or at least she was."

He stopped and turned again. "How long ago was that?"

"More than a month ago."

"Did you tell your grandfather?"

She shook her head. "Not until last night. I didn't want to. I was afraid he might be angry with me."

"Beat you?"

Her eyes widened. "No! Never. He was a good man. More like my father than any father I ever had. My mama, she ran away a long time ago." Tears glistened in her eyes, but she kept on. "Miss Meecher said to tell him she was okay and that she was just helping a friend, that she would be home soon and not to worry about her."

"What did she really say?"

"She told me to go, to get help, get the law. I told her I would. It was around back by the kitchens, she was cooking there. But . . ."

"Tita, what happened then? I have to know."

"We were heard by a man."

"One of the men from last night or today?"

"Yes, the one from today. Big Gabe, he called himself. He said if I did go to the law as I had promised Miss Meecher I would do, he would kill her first, then he would go to our house and kill Grandfather. Somehow he knew we were there. Grandfather had tried to keep me hidden, dressed me like a boy for a long time, but Miss Meecher finally told him to let me be a young woman. I was so glad when she said that. But look at what trouble being a woman brings. It is no fun, you know. No good at all."

"Why didn't you just tell me this when we were having dinner last night? Might've been able to . . ." He stopped himself, but the implication was there. They could have saved the old man's life, maybe even the lives of the four bandits. Who knew?

"I did not know you. I did not trust you. You weren't there, in the dark. Big Gabe . . . it was no good."

"Did he hurt you?"

"He did, yes. And the others. They said it was to make sure I would keep my mouth quiet about going to the law."

"What about last night with me? You seemed to trust me then."

"That sort of thing is different. It had nothing to do with anything else."

Slocum swung down from his horse and helped her down. This was a complex girl, no doubt.

A narrow stream of cool, clear water cut through thinning sage and scrubby pines. Slocum led the horses to it, let them drink their fill. He nodded to the girl and she crouched down, managing despite her bound hands, and sipped just upstream from the four horses. When she was finished, she stood and it seemed to Slocum that he was seeing her for the first time, the real Tita. She regarded him with a level gaze, no bitterness hidden in her eyes, no fake smile, no veiled villainy or anger.

Without taking his eyes from her, he slipped his Bowie knife from its sheath and sliced through the rope binding her wrists. "We need to work together on this thing."

She nodded and rubbed her chafed wrists, then soaked them in the stream. "Do you have a plan?" she said as she waggled her hands in the water, flexing her fingers.

He smiled and tossed her a strip of jerky, watching the horses as they nosed around the sparsely covered ground for something edible. "Me? A plan? I thought I might send you back to Minton, scare up some law. Meanwhile, I'll mosey on in there, see what's what."

"If you will excuse me for saying so, that's not much of a plan, John Slocum."

"You are free to make it into something we can both be

proud of—or at least something that might not get us both killed."

She chewed the tough leathery meat. "How about you take me in there as your prisoner? That would put you in good standing with the boss of the ranch."

"That would be that colonel, the one you referred to as a 'bastard,' if I recall."

"Yes, him. That way you will be one of the guards or whatever they have there—lots of men, that much I can tell you. They have lots of men with guns there."

"Great," said Slocum, rasping a hand across his stubbled jaw.

"It is as if they are guarding something of great value."

"I don't doubt that. Gold usually breeds men with guns like a thin hound breeds lice. Tell me, why would you want to do this? Give yourself over to them just like that?" He leaned close to her face, but she didn't flinch, didn't back away.

"You sure there isn't something you're forgetting to tell me?"

"John Slocum, I don't want to go to Minton to find the law. I don't think the law would listen to me. I think they would find all the dead men you've left behind and they would blame me, maybe even my grandfather. They might even blame us for Miss Meecher not being around. In case you haven't noticed, I am not like you, eh? I am a Mexican, and that means I am not treated the same way you are."

Slocum tightened the cinch on their saddles and said, "First it's being a woman that's so godawful, then it's being a Mexican. What's next with you, girl? You keep on like this, life will be nothing but one sour apple after another."

"I am not going back to the law alone. I don't care what you say."

"I could just tie you up and leave you here."

"You could, but you will not."

"Oh?" He leaned against his saddle. "And why not?"

"Because we have one more night on the trail and you will get cold. It is the way of all men."

He narrowed his eyes at her and swung up into the saddle. "Mount up. I want you riding in front of me."

"Of course you do."

"Hmm."

"You don't trust me?" she said as she rode by him.

"Not yet." He watched her back, then said, "Maybe I will later."

Ahead of him, facing forward, the girl smiled.

6

For the rest of the day, the girl gave Slocum no trouble, even offered a handful of half smiles and coquettish looks—all reasons that made him more inclined than ever to sleep with one eye open and the other one half-shut. He didn't make it this far as a wanted man since the war not to recognize when he was being strung along. This girl had more she wasn't telling—he just hoped it didn't get him into hot water once he got to the Triple T.

"We'll camp here," he said late in the day. They had descended into a misty little glade beside fresh water. It looked to be a spot others had used for just that purpose, though not in a while. Good thing, since the last thing he wanted was to be stumbled upon as they rested up for what he guessed was going to be a hard next day.

They spent a quiet time readying their meager camp, and built a decent cook fire since he reasoned unless they were overrun by a dozen emissaries from the ranch—the land of which they might well be on now anyway—he could probably talk his way out of whatever sticky situation might arise, if the girl played along. He still wasn't sure of her and her intentions. Since they made camp, she had left off being exceedingly nice and resumed a more moderate temperament, which suited Slocum just fine.

After a decent meal of biscuits, beans, bacon, and coffee, they discussed vague plans for the next day. It didn't much matter to Slocum what she had in mind, as long as she complied with what he wanted to do. She'd not proven herself to be trustworthy and he let her know such in no uncertain terms.

"Then I will go in as your prisoner, as I said earlier, and you can try to become one of them."

"The first part of that is what bothers me," he said, setting down his cup on a flat rock by the fireside. "What will you do once they have you in their hands, girl?"

"I can take care of myself, John Slocum." She poked at the fire with a stick.

"No, you'll pardon me for saying so, but I don't think you can. You are a kind young woman, but you are no match for them. If what you and your grandfather said is true, and I have less reason now than ever to doubt you, then we are talking about some mighty bad men. Men you don't want to fall in with again."

"You forget, I have already, as you say, 'fallen in with them.' Now it is just a matter of falling in again. It will be worth it if we can get Miss Meecher back. She's the only person I have left in the world who means anything to me. Do you understand that? Have you ever felt that way about anybody?"

Slocum looked at her for a long moment over the shimmering heat and drifting smoke of the small fire. Finally he said, "Yes, as a matter of fact, I have." Then he said no more, his mind for the moment irretrievably lost on a trail he'd not intentionally traveled very much at all in years.

His family, taken from him so long ago, and yet sometimes it felt like yesterday that he'd lost them. The war had a way of smearing itself into a person's life, of blotting out whole weeks and months and years. He wondered if other people who'd been through it felt the same way.

How did such things begin in the first place? Arguments among neighbors blossomed into bigger and broader disagreements until weapons were raised. And soon, people who wanted nothing more than to be left alone were caught up in the midst of the madness, too, and they were hurt . . . or worse.

"It's the innocent people who need the help every time," he said, almost in a whisper.

"What did you say?"

He spun on her, his hand already grabbing for a Colt. She had somehow crept close to him while he sat there like a fool, casting for old, worn-out memories and staring into the fire.

She drew back in alarm, her eyes showing genuine fear of him for the first time that he recalled. Innocent eyes, and his first reaction was to defend himself with violence. He settled the gun back in the leather. "I'm sorry about that. You startled me. I never heard you creep up like that."

"No, it is I who am sorry. I should not have come up to you like that, but you seemed so sad all of a sudden."

They sat like that for a few more minutes, then she shivered.

"Don't you have any more clothes?"

"I'm wearing them."

Slocum hopped up, and in a moment came back with his wool blanket, wrapped it around both their shoulders, and pulled her to him. She set her head on his chest and soon he heard her quiet, steady breathing that told him she had fallen asleep.

He didn't mind it in the least. It was a nice evening, stars were out, the horses were safe, his belly was full, and he had coffee at hand. A quirly would be nice, but he could forgo a trip to the saddlebag for that. He needed time to think things through. He'd never intended to ride into such a hornets' nest, but here he was, and there, up ahead at the ranch, were supposedly a whole lot of people who weren't able to help themselves. He had no idea what help he might offer them, but he had to try something. Anything would be better than letting them live as slaves.

The girl shifted in her sleep, brought a hand just under her chin. He pulled the blanket tight around her. It was a nice feeling. She seemed like a good person, pretty, intelligent, headstrong, and bent on some mission that she wasn't yet ready to tell him about, of that he felt sure. Maybe it was as simple as flat-out revenge. Maybe she really did just care for Marybeth that much. Lord knows she had that effect on people.

A finer woman than Marybeth Meecher he'd not come across in a long time. He'd thought of her often on the trail, wondering what life would have been like with her had he stayed on as she'd asked him to. He'd been sorely tempted and had remained with her for far longer than he'd intended at the outset.

But in the end, his fear of bringing his troubles as a wanted man to her doorstep led him to move on. He vowed to her he'd be back. But one thing let to another, and before he knew it, nearly three years had passed. Life had a way of doing that—entire months or years seemed to pass in a finger snap.

Just then a coyote wailed not that far off, then another closer in. Soon it seemed they had the camp ringed. The girl tensed, looked up at him. "Are we in danger?"

"Nah, they're just singing. To my mind, they are mostly musical creatures. Lots of folks will kill them just for the sake of killing them, but I like them. Good company on the trail when it's dark and lonely at night." He looked down at her, smiled. "As long as they don't get too friendly, that is. After all, they are wild creatures."

"Me, too, John Slocum." Her hand snaked down his belly and rested on the buttoned fly of his denims. "But you let me get close, eh?"

7

The next morning, they had forked leather and were pounding the dust trail an hour before sunrise, leftover biscuits and bacon in their hands. A bellyful of hot coffee was the one concession to slowing down—Slocum liked to start his day with hot coffee whenever possible, and today it just didn't seem to matter if they waited another twenty minutes for the coffee to boil.

"Do you always travel this way?"

"What way is that?" Slocum said through a mouthful of biscuit and bacon.

"Up early and going fast."

"Only way I know to keep one step ahead of whatever it is we're all trying to outrun in this life."

"You have a funny way of talking, John Slocum."

"So you said. Listen, I expect we'll be to the ranch headquarters before noon. Any of this look familiar to you? After all, you've been along here and I haven't."

"Yes, this is the way to the ranch. You should tie my hands before we get there and make sure you can explain the extra horses."

"I will, don't you worry. But I'm not going to lie."

"What do you mean?"

"I'm going to say I shot the men. They attacked us first, after all. Gave me no reason and no choice."

The girl said nothing, but Slocum noticed that she looked troubled and unsure of herself, something he'd not seen on her face before.

By midmorning, with a high sun and no breeze threatening a few more hot hours in the saddle, Slocum reined up and fetched his telescope from his saddlebag. He extended it and raised it to his eye. "Yep, a welcoming party, I'd say. Two men headed this way. Must have seen our dust."

He handed the device to the girl and she looked through it.

"I expect they'll be on us inside of twenty minutes. We best get you trussed up—if you're still up for it."

"Of course I am. It's too late now anyway."

"No, no, it's not. We could figure out something else."

"Like what?"

"I have no idea," he said, "but I'm sure something will occur to me."

She closed her eyes and sighed. "No, I must be seen to be your prisoner if this is to work."

"I don't like the idea of you going in there alone, as a captive. Those men aren't to be trusted—they'll try to hurt you."

"No, they won't. I know someone that will help protect me. Trust me, I can't explain it right now. But trust me. Besides, it is the fastest way I know of to get inside with the slaves. Only . . . promise me, John Slocum, that you will come for us." She looked away and Slocum realized that any odd behavior he'd seen in her since yesterday was probably nothing more than nervousness.

He tied her wrists and they didn't speak again until the riders came close enough that they could take in their appearance—the riders weren't impressive.

"For as vast and rich a ranch as this, you'd think the owner could afford a better caliber of man than what we've seen so far."

The first to ride up, a tall, reedlike man sitting ramrod straight on a bay, reined up to within ten feet of them. The other, a short, young man with a chaw bulge in his cheek, ambled up on a splay-legged buckskin. He spoke first. "What you doing here, mister? This here's Triple T land and you are trespassin'."

"Shut up, Harley." The thin man narrowed his eyes and looked past Slocum. "Looks like he's done more than trespass, looks like somehow he's got Gabe's and the Pole's horses in tow."

"And no Gabe nor Pole," said Slocum. "So those were their names."

The young, chubby ranch hand reached for his pistol. "What do you mean, 'were'? You didn't kill them, did you?"

Slocum already had his Colt drawn and sat shaking his head.

The older, thin man watched all this. "Leave it be, Harley. I'll do the talking, you do the shuttin' up. How 'bout it, mister? How you come to have possession of their horses? Where they at?"

"About a day's ride south of here, laid out on the hillside where they ambushed us."

The tall man didn't show much emotion, just sat there regarding Slocum and the girl. Harley, behind him, had turned a deep shade of purple and worked his chaw in a furious manner. Finally the tall man said, "The girl. I seen her before. Why's she trussed up?"

"Tried to kill me."

"Sounds like everyone's out to get you."

"That's a truth, I haven't been having the best run of luck lately. Far as the girl goes, I had no choice. I'd come too far to take her back to the law." Slocum glanced at her. "And she's too pretty to shoot, so I brung her along, figured that with a ranch the size of the Triple T, there might well be some sort of use for such a creature as this. Scullery maid or some such."

The pudgy youth sluiced a long rope of brown chew juice, then dragged a cuff across his begrimed whiskers. "Oh, we'll find something for her to do, you can bet on that."

"I just bet you will. Just so you know, she stays with me. I don't find the job I was promised once I get to the ranch, we're leaving together. She may have tried to kill me, but she has her uses."

"What's this about a job?" Harley glared at Slocum.

"Harley, is it? Do as the man says and shut up."

The thin man nodded, almost smiled, then said, "So what's this about a job?"

"No offense, friend, but unless you're the owner of this here ranch, I suggest we just get moving along. I am expected."

The man's jaw muscles tightened but he nodded, flicked a finger toward Harley, and said, "That side. I'll ride here, beside Mr. . . ."

"And it's a pleasure to meet you, too," said Slocum, not offering his name. The tall man didn't press it.

They rode for another hour. The only sounds were the horses' shod hooves occasionally striking a stone, the creak of worn saddle leather, the soft rubbery snort of a horse blowing. Anytime Slocum glanced at Harley, the chunky youth had his eyes focused on Tita's bobbing breasts. He was going to be trouble—and there was probably a whole bunkhouse full of Harleys up ahead. Slocum regretted agreeing to the girl's plan, but now there truly was no way out of it. They had to go forward. He hoped like hell she had something up her sleeve that she wasn't telling him about. Or she was going to have a rough time of it.

When the ranch came into view, it was as impressive as Slocum had been led to believe. The buildings were all painted white, stick-built, not log—at least the fronts. And the ranch house itself was a massive affair with columns and two full verandahs that would look more at home down South, where he'd spent his youth in Georgia. He did note that everything looked as though it could use a fresh coat of paint.

A third rider rode out to meet them and halted them at a second decorative gate that led to the buildings proper. He was a well-muscled, tousle-haired man who Slocum was sure was a hit with the ladies even when he wasn't trying to be. He kept glancing back over his shoulder. Slocum followed his sightline and saw, beyond the barns, a four-mule team pulling a heavy, shrouded wagon away from the buildings toward the craggy low peaks in the near distance.

Closer in, all about them, the land was browned, the grass a scraggly thatch of ungrazed pastureland. He saw no cow pies, no hoofprints, no signs of the vast herds of cattle a ranch this size should rightfully be running. His discovery and subsequent confusion must have been writ large on his face, despite his efforts to appear nonchalant. The thin man said, "Cattle been moved to higher grazing. We got a lot of land here."

Slocum raised an eyebrow, half nodded.

Slim took that to mean skepticism. "They're around, don't you worry about it."

Once the distant tarped work wagon had rumbled and creaked well beyond the ranch into the distance, the handsome cowboy jerked his head toward the ranch house. "Come on then."

They drew up to a steel hitch rail before the grand house, which looked to Slocum even more imposing than it had from a half-mile back. A smallish man, stout and dressed in a cotton-color linen suit, and with white hair and a trimmed dagger beard, all seemingly suited to go with the look of the house, descended the steps slowly, his white leather shoes making a gritty scuffing noise with each slow step. He kept his eyes on the motley assortment of riders before him.

"Look sharp," hissed Handsome. "It's Colonel Mulletson."

A true Old Southern colonel, eh? thought Slocum. Odder and odder.

After the thin man made explanations as to how he'd found Slocum and the girl, the colonel eyed them a silent moment more, then said, "And just how did you hear about our humble operation, Mr. . . . aaah, what was the name again?" He squinted up at Slocum as if what he was about to tell him was perhaps the most important thing he ever would hear.

"Slocum. John Slocum."

"That's it!" The colonel snapped his fingers and nodded.

"And I heard about the Triple T from a friend down Dodge. Name of Rufus, you might remember him? Older fella with a limp, worn out from prospecting, but his looks don't slow him none. He can still move cattle like he was in his prime. He heard from someone else in town, I forget who just now, that your ranch was in sore need of hands and that such a place would surely, given its size, be able to use someone such as myself. My credentials come hard won, but they're honest."

A snort rose behind him. He didn't have to turn around to know it was Harley. He'd give a month's wages to wipe that smirk off the chubby young fool's face with a knuckle or two. And something told him the opportunity would arise sooner than later.

A round of sharp stares from Colonel Mulletson and the other cowhands stifled the young whelp's mirth.

"You said you were expected." The thin hand who'd met them glared at Slocum.

"If I hadn't, would you have brought me here?"

The colonel emitted a short laugh. "Initiative. I like that in an employee. No need to sell me on your abilities, Mr. Slocum. Any fool—even I—can tell just by the look of you that you know your way around a ranch. And I daresay you may find yourself impressed with the range of skills required of my employees. Compensation is fair, I don't think any gathered here will argue that, and for that I require hard work and tight lips." He stepped toward Slocum's horse and his face grew grave. "For instance, I will not tolerate talk of our affairs beyond the boundaries of this ranch. Do we understand each other, Mr. Slocum?"

"Sounds fair to me, Colonel."

"Now, if you are interested, Mr. Slocum, I'd like to talk with you about how you feel you can best serve me. In fact, I find I am in need of a . . . shall we say, a wrangler, at present. But there are caveats."

"For instance?" said Slocum.

"You must do exactly what you are told. I will not tolerate insubordination."

"There are all sorts of ways of interpreting that word, Colonel, aren't there?"

"Maybe so, Mr. Slocum, but as long as you forget all of them but my way, we'll get along swimmingly well."

Slocum thought the man was surely hiding something. The whole thing—the job, the work itself, the other hands loafing about the place, and not asking to check a man's references, nor at least inquiring about them before the man even dismounted, all this was odd and some of it unheard of. Still, it all began to sound as if the girl and her grandfather were right.

Handsome cleared his throat and waited for the colonel to favor him with a glance. "Sir, as I'm sure you noticed, this here fella's got Gabe's and the Pole's horses and gear."

"But no Gabe and Pole, eh?" Colonel Mulletson knitted his brow in mock concern.

"No, Colonel," said Slocum. "That is the truth of it. As I told Slim and Harley here when they first come upon us, those two boys didn't give us much warning before they opened up on us. It was all I could do to incapacitate them."

"Well, why forever didn't you bring their bodies back on their own horses?"

"One of them was too fat for me to heft, the other was too rank. Smelled like the southbound end of a northbound moose."

Colonel Mulletson nodded knowingly, but Slocum could tell by the looks on the cowhands' faces that he would have to answer to them on their own terms for killing their compadres. Should word of the other two get out, he'd have even more to deal with.

"Well, we were down two men, but now it appears"—the colonel waved a hand at the two sullen-looking riderless horses standing hipshot behind the rest—"that we are now down four men. But with the addition of Mr. Slocum here, we'll surely regain any ground we may have lost due to vacant souls."

Colonel Mulletson turned his attention to the girl. "Now, what have we here?" He made no pretense of hiding the fact that he was looking her up and down, from hair to feet and back, stopping at a few points along the way, detouring around and through certain hills and valleys of her physical terrain.

Slocum said, "This is . . . you know, I still don't know her name, and after she tried to up and rob me. Funny thought, I almost don't want to know. She's a tough little nut, I tell you what. But she can cook and . . . a few other things. As I told your advance party here, I had come too far to turn back and bring her to the law. I figured you all might find a use for her here at such a famous and sizable spread as this."

"What say you, girl?" The paunchy little colonel patted

his belly, setting his gold watch chain to jingling, but his look to her was stern.

For the first time, all eyes were on Tita's face. Slocum thought maybe she enjoyed having the attention, even if it was from rank men.

"I wasn't trying to hurt Mr. Slocum," she said. "I only wanted food. It had been a long time since I ate and I was beginning to feel like I could not go on much longer. And then he came along. I was afraid he would pass me by, so I tried to surprise him."

"To take his food," said the colonel, nodding as if he understood completely. Judging from the size of his ample gut, it seemed he did. The colonel thrust out his bottom jaw, rubbed his dagger beard, and nodded, as if agreeing with an unseen guest.

"And he says you can cook, eh?"

The girl nodded, looking for all the world eager to repent a sinful past and take up wholesome ways. Slocum almost laughed.

"Good, good," said their fat host. "We always have use of another hand in the kitchen." He looked up at Slocum. "I'll turn her over to our head cook's custody. She will no doubt appreciate a hand with the cooking and . . . whatnot."

He turned to the girl, still seated in the saddle, and set a hand on her thigh. "Provided you mind your p's and q's, eh?" This struck the colonel as funny and he bent double with laughter, a pinched whinnying sound that Slocum thought would be embarrassing if it ever came out of his own mouth.

The man's hands all began their own variation on the noise, until Colonel Mulletson stood upright, suddenly stone-faced, and stared them down. He turned his gaze on Slocum next, and his genial smile returned. "I figure, Slocum, that since you are new here, we ought to get acquainted. I can tell you about the Triple T, what our goals are, that sort of thing. Why don't you let the boys show you the bunkhouse—you can get settled in there. We have a couple of hours yet to supper, but I'll tell the cook to put on a good feed, something memorable."

"You make it sound like the last supper, Colonel." Slocum slid a smile on his stubbly face.

Again, the man guffawed, then said, "Not at all, sir. Not at all. Just the first of many, I hope."

"How about I get one of the men to show me around the spread, get the lay of the place. I'm sure you have a fresh horse I can use."

"All in good time, young man. All in good time. For now, why don't you kick back and enjoy a cool drink of spring water? We'll cover all the ground you'll want to in short order. In fact, you may just grow tired of seeing so much of this ranch!"

"What about the girl?" said Slocum, his gut knotting tight but not wanting to show it.

The colonel had already headed toward the broad steps, but stopped and turned back. "As I said, I'll show her to the cook and she can take it from there." He offered a hand to Tita to help her down from her horse. "Bring your belongings and I'll escort you to meet our cook. You'll love her and I daresay you will find her to be a fair supervisor."

As Tita held out her bound hands to Slocum to once again slice through the rope binding her wrists, she looked at him, just a hint of smugness in her eyes.

Slocum wagged the long blade of his Bowie knife in her face. "Now you mind the colonel here, and the cook, too. By bringing you along, you are my responsibility. Any stepping out of line you do here will reflect poorly on me, and that isn't something I am likely to look on favorably, you hear?"

Slocum laid it on thick, and the girl narrowed her eyes accordingly. He didn't think it was an act on her part. Despite the urgings of the other men, Slocum sat his horse and waited for the girl to disappear into the big house with Colonel Mulletson. Then he nudged the Appaloosa forward and headed to the bunkhouse.

8

They rode across the vast yards to the bunkhouse—a multi-level affair with fancy walkways and porches out front, and a path leading to the four-door privy out back. Slocum marveled once again at how well kept the place looked, but also how barren it felt. The Triple T lacked all the usual signs of a busy, working ranch—no bawling of calves looking for their mothers, no constant boil of dust from scattered head in the distance, no hay ricks, none of it. Most of all, he missed the distinct dry tang of cattle smells floating on the air.

"Where are all the stock?"

Slim said, "You were already told that."

"Yeah, just you shut your mouth and we'll do the askin'." He didn't have to look to know it was Harley.

Slocum looked behind him to see the young man glaring at him. Great, I trade one angry youngster for another. For once, though, he noticed that his fellow cowhands didn't shout him down and tell him to keep his mouth shut. Harley noticed it, too. He spat tobacco juice and sat a little straighter in the saddle.

They reined up at the hitch rail in front of the bunkhouse and Slocum said, "I'd like to take care of my horse and the girl's, too, before I tend to myself."

"Nope," said Handsome. "Harley here'll take 'em to the

barn. Don't you worry. He may be an idiot, but he don't mistreat animals. Ain't that right, Harley?"

Slocum made to reach to his breast pocket for his makin's, but he wanted his hand free for clearing leather should it come to that. "Thanks just the same, fella, but I reckon I'll take care of my own horse my own self. Always have, always will."

From just behind him, to his left, he heard Slim say, "First time for everything."

Slocum reached for his Colt, felt the ebony handle just under his fingertips, and he was jerked hard by the shirt collar and felt himself plunging from the saddle. He managed to yank his left boot free of the stirrup—knowing that the Appy would crow-hop if given half the chance, and drag him from here to hell and back around the yard, just for the fun of it.

Slocum had not expected being pulled from the saddle. He landed hard and with one thing on his mind: what these gents had planned for him.

Slocum sprang up from the dust, the Appy dancing just behind him. He'd lost his hat; it sat at his feet, the crown dented in. He didn't care. His trail clothes were already dusted, but now felt as though they'd been filled with the stuff before he slipped into them.

As the dust cleared, he saw Handsome and Slim had both dismounted and standing before him, their sidearms drawn.

Slocum stood still, his legs planted shoulder-width apart, his hands ready to draw his hip guns. He was breathing hard and he felt a tingling in his left shoulder where he'd landed, trying to roll with it. "Now, Slim," he said, catching his breath and blowing the dust from his mouth and nose. "That wasn't a very kind thing to do to someone you'll be working with, was it?"

The tall, thin man peeled back the hammer on his pistol. "The last thing on my mind is being kind to you, Slocum."

"Well now," said Slocum, making what he hoped was a slow play for his gun. "Just what is on your mind, then, Slim?"

"The interesting fact that four of our friends have not returned, and yet about when we were expecting them, why, you turn up instead. And with that little Mexican squeezebox to boot." He clicked the hammer back to the deadly position.

"And my name's not Slim. It's Everett. Call me Slim again and I'll plug you, and be glad for it."

Handsome waved his pistol back and forth at Slocum. "Get that gun belt and knife off, but slow, two fingers, and let it drop."

From behind him, Slocum heard Harley giggle. "What are you two fixin' to do with him anyway?"

Precisely what Slocum was wondering.

Everett barked again at the boy. "Get those damn horses to the barn." He looked at Slocum. "And treat their horses right. I hear you've done anything less than that and you'll be answering to me, you got that, Harley?"

"Aw, you know I won't hurt a horse, Everett, even if it does belong to a killer."

They all waited, poised in the dusty yard before the bunkhouse like they were in some bizarre dance. They heard the horses being led away, then Handsome said, "That's right, Slocum. We know what you are. We'd bet money you killed our friends and that you are here for a take, ain't that right?"

"Clew, you have got a mouth that will get you in trouble one day soon."

Slocum watched warring emotions play on Handsome's face. Apparently he was named Clew.

"Is that was the colonel meant about loose lips, boys?" Slocum looked at each of them. They weren't happy.

"Inside, now!" Clew took a step closer, but Everett stopped him. "Don't get close to him, just let the gun do the directing, boy." As if demonstrating, he waved his pistol at Slocum, who reluctantly obliged.

They all clumped up on to the porch with Slocum in front, holding his hands up, though not too high. He guessed there probably wasn't anyone else in the bunkhouse; otherwise with all the ruckus they would have been out by now spectating.

He decided he'd use the dark of the room and the time it took their eyes to adjust to hit them hard and gain the upper hand. He wasn't so sure of his odds of living out the day here at the Triple T, especially if these yahoos were convinced that he had killed their friends. While it was true he'd ushered them to their deaths, but he didn't really have a choice.

Somehow he didn't think that would mean all that much to either of them.

He took one, two steps into the dim interior. Off to the right, against a long back wall, he saw a squat black steel stove, silver adornments atop. His eye, however, was not set on taking in the fine amenities of the bunkhouse, but rather on something he might be able to use as a weapon against these two gunhands.

Slocum's eyes settled again on the stove against the back wall of the room. The cast-iron removable lid handle would do nicely—except for the fact that it was all the way across the room and he wasn't. Yet.

Clew was the first through the door just behind Slocum. "Keep it moving, Slocum, to the middle of the room. We got talking to do."

Slocum kept his hands half-raised, but bent low and pivoted, bringing his left leg up high. "I've had about enough talk for one day," he said through gritted teeth just before his arching boot caught Clew just under his jutting square jaw.

Slocum felt the man's teeth come together hard, heard the man groan, and a couple of somethings—teeth?—cracked and snapped. He went down not as Slocum had hoped—backward—but fell like a chopped tree onto his left side. His handgun flipped from his grasp and spun into the shadows under a table covered in playing cards, poker chips, and a peach tin someone had used as an ash tray.

Slocum followed through with his kick and dropped himself almost flat to the floor. The pistol had gone to the far side of the room. He'd have to cross in front of the open door to get at it. He risked a glance at Clew, and saw that the man lay slumped on his side, just as he fell, not even moaning. Out cold.

At the first sign of a scuffle inside, Everett jumped back out of the doorway. Now, judging from his shadow, Slocum saw that the man stood just to the right of the doorway. If Slocum's guess was right, Everett was no green hand. He was a seasoned old dog who wouldn't wait around outside wondering what to do.

If Slocum were Everett, he'd know that the longer he

waited out there, the greater the chance that Slocum could arm himself—if he hadn't already—and would be waiting for him to make his play. But he doubted the man would use his gun. They'd just wanted to rough Slocum up for killing their two friends. What would they do if they knew for sure he'd killed four of them?

Time for me to oblige him, thought Slocum. He dove forward, rolled onto his right shoulder through the light slanting into the middle of the room from the doorway, and came to a halt on the far side of the row of wooden chairs. The gun had to be under the table somewhere. He lifted a chair, eased it out of the way, and groped in the dark for the pistol. Splitting his thoughts between grabbing hold of a snake and grabbing hold of the pistol, Slocum finally felt the reassuring touch of cold steel beneath his grasping fingers.

"Slocum! You gone crazy in there? We only wanted to talk."

"Yeah, I know what you mean by that. Your method of talk involves buttoning up my eyes with a few punches and kicks. You and your boys best get one thing straight—I didn't force those fools to attack me. They thought of that shiny plan all on their own."

"That don't matter. I'm top dog of this outfit and you would do well to keep that in mind."

"Colonel Mulletson will find that of interest, I'm sure."

"That's how it's going to be, then, huh?"

"I reckon so. You set it up, don't forget that. I'm the new boy."

Slocum heard a sigh, then a hammer being eased off. Finally, Everett stepped into the doorway, skylined within it. With the light leaking in around him, the tall man looked larger than life.

"Okay then." The man made a point of shoving his pistol into his holster in full view of Slocum, who he still couldn't see in the room. "Enough of this. Help me prop Clew up, see how bad you hurt him."

Slocum slid out from behind the table, stood with the pistol in his hand. "You'll forgive me for not setting this down just yet. I haven't exactly received a rosy welcome from you all."

Everett sighed again and strode into the room, his hands

hovering chest level. "Now hold on, just take 'er easy. You knew half of what goes on here, you'd understand why we're all fired up to make sure you're who you say you are. You got to see things from our point of view." He bent to Clew, slapped the man's face roughly a couple of times. "Wake up, Clew! Wake up!"

A thin wheeze drizzled out of the prone man's broken mouth, then his eyes fluttered open. He pulled in a deep breath through his nose and pushed himself up. His head wobbled and Everett helped steady him. The injured man looked up and focused his crazy eyes on Slocum, standing above him smiling with the man's own pistol in his hand.

"Whaa . . . ? What are you . . . ? You!" But his words came out thick and wet, as if he were talking through wet flannel.

"Yes, Clew, it's still me. Now, Everett, what were you saying about your point of view? That is, before we were so rudely interrupted."

"No call to goad him, Slocum. You done kicked his teeth in, ain't that enough?"

Clew shrugged Everett's helping hands away and struggled to his knees. Then his hands went to his mouth and he let out a gagging cry at what he found there, as if his hand had slipped into a pot of scalding water and the pain were only now beginning to pulse at full throb.

"You thon of a bitch! You buth-ted my teeth!"

Slocum eased off the hammer and flipped the pistol up in the air. He caught it by the barrel. "And you were just going to give me a stern talking to, is that it?" He pulled back with the gun. "How'd you like me to relocate that pretty nose, give you a matched set?"

"Easy, Slocum! Dammit, man. You are either certified loco or you're setting yourself up to seem like someone we shouldn't offend."

"That's up to you to decide. Now, all I came here for was a job, and all I got since I started on this trip was attacked by a girl and bushwhacked by thugs—who, it turns out, work here. Just why had they strayed so far from the ranch anyway? No, never mind, tell me later. And then, when I get here, you and your cronies treat me like—"

"Like what, you athhole?" Clew shouted on his way wobbling to the table. "Like the man who gunned down our two friendth?"

Slocum flopped open the pistol's cylinder, thumbed out the shells, and let them drop to the floor. Then he tossed the pistol onto the table and said to Everett, "You fellas still want to talk, I'm partial to a cup of hot coffee while I palaver. I have a while before I'll be summoned to supper up to the big house. I'll be back presently. I'm going to go check on my horse, clean up. Keep Smiley here on a short leash or I won't be responsible for his actions—or my reactions."

Slocum walked outside, stepped away from the direct line of fire out the door, just in case Everett decided to have a change of heart. Though the man seemed the type to reason out his thinking, the next few seconds would tell. Slocum snatched up his gun belt and strapped it on, facing the empty doorway. But nobody followed him out, and more important, no bullets did. He grabbed his hat on the way by and banged the dust off it.

Then Slocum strode to the barn that looked most likely to house horses. He kept a hand on the butt of a Colt, and under his low-tugged hat brim, he surveyed the buildings. It didn't appear as if there were all that many folks about. Where would they all be on such an afternoon? At the gold mine Tita and her grandfather swore existed?

First things first, Slocum, he told himself. Let's get the saddlebags, fresh duds, and a spiffing, then talk with the gents back at the bunkhouse. Then hit the big house for a feed and get some more questions answered.

As he reached for the leather strap handle of what he took to be the tack room door, a horse's whinny sounded out, though muffled, as if it were stifled somehow.

He couldn't tell you why, but it triggered deep-seated reflexes that made Slocum pull and thumb back the hammer on his Colt. There—a scuffling inside, sounds of a nervous horse stomping, nickering, and again, sounds of struggle.

He didn't need to hear more than those two seconds' worth of sounds. Slocum whipped open the door and leveled off, standing askance and peering into the darkened gloom of the stable. Great, he thought, another dim building. He pulled in a deep draught of air through his nose and stepped, light-footed, over the threshold. Far in the back of the barn, he heard more struggling, a horse nervously whickering. The Appaloosa, for certain. No other horse he'd heard lately sounded so throaty when agitated. What was going on?

Stick to the shadows, he told himself, and skirt the main room. The sounds intensified from what appeared to be a stall in a back corner. The closer Slocum drew, the more the sounds ticked him off. Was that damn Harley kid hurting his horse?

Whoever it was, and he bet money that it was the annoying, cud-chewing Harley, he didn't think the kid had heard him yet. Slocum cat-footed around the edge of the open center of the stable until he got to the half-dark stall where the sounds were coming from. It was definitely the Appaloosa—he'd know those angry churning sounds anywhere. But they still sounded muffled somehow.

Again he leveled off, stood just outside the door frame, pistol aimed, and saw Harley looking intently into the feed trough. Poking up just above it, he spied the edge of his saddlebags. The boy was rummaging through his things.

"See you didn't bother to wait for me, Harley."

The young man spun, guilt and surprise on his pudgy face. His hands were still both in the trough.

"Raise them up high, boy. Slow or I'll make damn sure you won't have anything to raise ever again."

When the boy had done so, Slocum cut his eyes past Harley to the shadows, and saw his horse had been snubbed tight to a ring in the wall, rough rope passed around his muzzle three or four wraps' worth. The horse was breathing hard and weals from fresh lashings had been raised on his neck and shoulder. Slocum's saddle lay in a heap in the corner of the stall.

"Well now, looks to me like you've been giving my horse a royal welcome, eh?"

"It ain't like that. We just needed to know you ain't someone who . . ."

"Someone who what, Harley?" Slocum flashed the boy a kindly uncle-like smile.

"Nothin'."

Slocum advanced on him, and the boy stumbled backward into the horse, which lashed out with a hobbled rear foot. Its stunted blow did little more than graze the boy's chunky leg.

"Are you saying that you didn't lash my horse there? That you didn't tie his mouth like that?"

"I . . . I don't know what you're talking about. He come in here just the way he was given to me."

"First of all, he was not given to you. But that's neither here nor there. Now, about my gear."

"I—I was just trying to fit it all back in there. I took it off the horse and set it in there, but it all spilled out. I was just tryin—"

"Yes, so you said. I'll tell you what, you strip down to your longhandles and toss your gear in a pile there on the floor."

"What? I ain't—"

Slocum cocked back the Colt all the way. "You will and Mr. Colt here says so."

When he'd finished, Slocum located a length of unused rope, presumably the piece that the boy had used to whip the Appaloosa. Slocum strapped Harley's arms tight behind him, and when Harley started to protest and yell, he tapped the boy hard on the temple with the barrel of the pistol. That shut him up for a few seconds. Slocum lashed the lad's socked feet together for good measure.

"Boy, anyone ever tell you about bathing? Maybe darning your socks? You are a pitiful rig." He snatched up the boy's bandanna from the stack of clothes and tied it tight around the boy's mouth. "Keep your head still or I'll really rap you on the bean, you hear me?"

Once he'd bound the kid, Slocum said, "Now comes the fun part." First, he gathered up his spilled possessions from the bottom of the trough, stuffed them in the saddlebags, and set them and his saddle, rifle, and boot outside the stall. Then he cut the ropes from the Appaloosa's muzzle and calmed the horse. Every few seconds he glanced at Harley and raised his eyebrows. The kid had begun whimpering around the bandanna gagging his mouth, and snot and tobacco juice spooled from the sides of his mouth.

"Now," said Slocum, once he'd massaged the horse and rubbed him down with a handful of hay. "My horse looks to have been ill treated in this, your establishment. I don't like to see that happen to any animal, most of all to my own horse. And I am damn sure that the horse is none too pleased with the strapping he received." Slocum slipped free the last rope tethering the Appaloosa to the ring in the wall. Then he cut the rope binding the kid's feet, and headed for the stall door.

The kid bellowed his fear and rage into the tightly wrapped bandanna, his face purpling, his nose running, and the veins on his neck and forehead bulging. As soon as Slocum slammed shut the stall door and jammed a handy length of planking into the wooden lift latch to keep it shut from the outside, the kid ran to the door, kicking and ramming into the high wooden enclosure.

Slocum hefted his gear, touched his hat brim to the staring, screaming boy, and headed for the front of the barn. Behind him, he heard the Appaloosa's throaty whinnies, felt the thud of his hooves as he gave the youth what for.

Slocum didn't think the kid would be killed, just roughed up a bit. He hadn't tied the kid's wrists too tight behind him, but it would take him a few frantic minutes before he'd free himself. Meanwhile, the Appaloosa was sure to chase him around the stall, take his pound of flesh for Harley's unwarranted mistreatment.

Slocum hefted his saddle up onto a rack. As he strolled back to the bunkhouse with his rifle and saddlebags, Slocum couldn't help whistling. The day hadn't worked out at all as he'd thought it might—much worse, in fact—but somehow he was in a good mood. He'd take it for now. Something told him it might be the last time he'd feel this way for a while.

9

Much to his surprise, when Slocum reentered the bunkhouse, he was greeted by the heavenly scent of fresh coffee and two seated cowboys.

"Everett, Clew." He nodded to them and noted that only one of them seemed relaxed and enjoying his coffee. Clew looked better than he had, but still seemed as if he wanted to launch himself across the table and kill Slocum. As a precaution, Slocum kept the thong free of his Colt's hammer. It wouldn't do to be ambushed again. He found a clean tin cup and poured himself some of the thick, aromatic liquid. But he stayed standing by the stove, his back to a wall, his eyes focused on the two seated men.

"So," he said, sipping the hot coffee. "Seems to me there's more *and* less to this outfit than meets the eye. I just bumped into Harley at the stable. He's fine by the way. He'll be along shortly. Tied up with work, dealing with an unruly horse."

Slocum bent his head forward and spoke in a lowered tone, "He was saying how the whole cattle operation here has seen better days, claims there's something bigger and better than cattle—his words, not mine. You'd never hear me utter such blasphemy. After all, we are on one of the West's biggest and most famous ranches, am I right, boys?"

"Thut up, Thlocum. You'll get yours, you wait and thee."

64

Slocum set down his cup and moved closer to the table. "I'm sorry, were you trying to speak, Clew? I didn't quite understand what you were saying. Sounded sort of thick and unclear."

"That's enough, Slocum." Everett set his cup down and placed both hands palm down on the tabletop. "You got any questions for us, I wish you'd up and ask 'em. I'm a direct sort of man."

"Fine." He eyed Everett, who seemed to be daring him to ask the obvious—was the ranch a front for a gold mine? And more important, were they using slave labor to get the ore out of the ground? But something told Slocum not to ask those questions just yet. If he did, then the girl could be in trouble and as well as Marybeth Meecher. Not to mention the lives of however many people the man had abducted and forced into slavery. If he blew his chances now, he might never get the opportunity to find out about them all. And right now, he was their only hope—a thin one, to be sure, but at least it was there.

"I guess what I want to know is," he said, sipping his coffee again. "Because I'm a cowman. Have been for a long, long time, always will be, I expect." He smiled at the two seated men. "Where in the hell are all the cattle? And why is everyone around here so dang hostile toward me? All I want to do is wrangle beeves on the land of this legendary ranch. Been waiting a long time to see this place, and now I see what my old far-ranging friend Rufus meant when he said that it was a land of golden opportunity, rich with potential."

He let his last couple of phrases sink in, watched the faces of the two men over the rim of his cup. If they'd absorbed his mild double meanings, they didn't let on.

Finally Everett spoke up: "Oh, we got cattle. As I said earlier, they been moved to higher ground, some other pastures and fields and whatnot. We was just about to bring some to these here fields you seen when you rode up. I expect we'll tend to that tomorrow."

Fields? Whatnot? He had figured that Everett, if not a full-bore cattleman, at least was someone who'd been around beeves enough to know the lingo. But he'd talked as if he spent his life running a trapline or playing poker. Either option was probably closer to the truth than him being a wrangler.

Slocum thought he'd give it one more try, and launched into a flurry of questions: "Anyone here know how big a herd you're running? Where's it located? How big is the range? What pastures are they in now?" But question after question passed, unknown and unrecognized, on their ignorant faces. He received no satisfactory responses, and that made him more certain than ever.

Finally, Everett drained his coffee cup, and said, "Slocum, a piece of free advice: Just go with the flow of things around here. Don't spoil a good thing for everyone. It will all be revealed in due course."

Slocum didn't really know what to say. They weren't inclined to tell him anything. A brief silence hung in the air of the dim little room where not long before he'd been sure he was going to be gutted or at least worked over pretty hard.

"Well, boys, as edifying as this has been, and believe me it's been most eye-opening—and I don't just mean the coffee—I expect it's about time for me to hit the wash basin and spiff up myself for a feed up to the big house. Are you all invited?"

Clew shifted his bloodshot eyes from staring at the table-top to Slocum's face. "No, no," came his muddy voice, the sarcasm still evident even through his garbled speech and puffy lips. "You go on ahead and enjoy yourthelf. We'll be here when you get back. Don't worry."

"But don't stay out too late," said Everett, settling his chair back down on four legs from leaning back against the wall. "We got a big day ahead of us tomorrow."

Both men looked at each other and smiled.

Slocum shook his head in amazement at the pair of them, but decided to let sleeping dogs lie. "Okay then. I'll clean up and head out. I'll bring you back some spuds and gravy."

They were silent as they watched him leave. "I hate him," said Clew when Slocum had left the room. "Tho bad I want to kill him with my bare handth."

"And I bet the colonel will let you do just that before this thing is over, but right now we need all the fresh workers we can get to fill that quota. I have a feeling something's going to change soon. The colonel's been acting odd. Always does when something's about to happen. Something to do with money." Everett looked around at the room, the doorway behind him, then leaned in close to Clew and lowered his voice. "And if we don't keep everything rolling, you know we'll take the blame."

Clew nodded, wincing at the throbbing pain leaching upward throughout his face. "I ain't about to let that happen."

"Me either," said Everett. "'Cause the colonel said we all got too much riding on this deal. Said we'd all be rich one day."

Just outside the door, Slocum waited a few more seconds before stepping carefully away. He'd hoped they thought he had made a beeline for the outdoor washing station, and that they might run their mouths. And they did. It was all starting to add up. Slow and steady.

Twenty minutes later, he'd washed himself, and donned a clean shirt and kerchief, dusted his trail pants, and dragged his fingers through his hair. He figured he'd check on the Appaloosa on his way to the house.

He nearly made it to the barn door when it swung outward and there before him stood a considerably reddened Harley. His face had been worked over, and was now puffing. And he limped and held one of his arms before him as if it were broken or strained.

"How you keepin', wrangler?" Slocum couldn't resist.

"I'll tell you what . . . you keep to your own self and I'll do the same. You won't be here long anyways."

Slocum strode right up to him, snatched the button front of his faded pink longhandles. "What do you mean by that, Harley?"

The boy winced, tried to pull away, but Slocum's hands gripped the soiled garment like bolted steel. "I . . . I just mean that anyone as . . . ornery as you . . . won't last long. That's all I meant, really."

Slocum shook his head, let go of the kid, and pushed past him to the barn. Over his shoulder, he said, "I assume my horse has been fed and watered."

There was no answer.

"I didn't think so. I expect you're still a little afraid of him. I understand. I'd be afraid of any animal that left me looking like you do." He smiled and walked into the cool of the barn.

Other than needing a feed and some water, the horse was in surprisingly good shape. The lash marks he'd seen earlier were already receding, and the marks on his nose from the wrapped rope were looking better than Slocum expected they would. Another few days and they'd all be gone.

The horse wasn't quite settled down, so Slocum spent a few minutes with him, gave him a bate of feed, a few forkfuls of hay. It was not decent-quality stuff, but considering the state of affairs here, he was glad to find anything edible for the horse. As long as it didn't make his horse ill while they were here, he didn't care much. He'd turn him out in the morning.

He poked around the rest of the stable, but saw no sign of the girl's chestnut, nor the two dead men's mounts. A nicker from outside, beyond the far end of the barn, led him out back, where he saw the three horses, plus a few others—some he recognized as those ridden by Everett, Clew, and Harley. With his mind at rest about that, he headed to the front door of the fancy house and mounted the steps.

The big burgundy double doors swung inward just as he reached for the brass horseshoe knocker. A tall, thin, white-haired man in a spotless black suit and white gloves stood before him. Only the man's eyes moved, and they beetled up and down Slocum's entire height before making eye contact.

"Welcome, sir. You are expected."

He nodded and walked on in. The man stood before him with his gloved hands outstretched. For a moment, Slocum wrinkled his brow, then saw the man's eyes glance toward his hat, and Slocum slipped off the sweat-stained topper. He nodded, smiled, and plopped the hat, crown down, into the man's waiting hands. "Thank you, sir. And may I say that suit is a most dapper-looking rig."

The man squinted briefly, then almost smiled, but not quite. Slocum shrugged and admired what views of the sumptuous home he could glean from standing in the foyer. Before him rose a wide stairwell with a massive cherrywood carved newel post that curved like a coiled snake upward into a long, graceful handrail. It was polished to a high, glowing gleam, like all the wood paneling and adornments. Everything glowed in the warm lamplight. High above, a crystal chandelier reflected the light in a million directions all at once.

With a curt command, the dapper gent he took to be the butler bade Slocum follow him to yet another set of tall, paneled doors. The man swung them wide to reveal a richly appointed formal dining room, dominated in the center by a long polished table set with polished silverware, crystal, and lit silver candlesticks.

"Well, Mr. Slocum, so nice of you to make it." Colonel Mulletson emerged through what looked to be a secret panel in the wall of the dining room. By the way he took slow, measured pains to pretend to conceal it, Slocum guessed that, as a big child would, the man wanted him to know it was a secret door.

"Not at all, it was kind of you to invite me. Though I see there are only two places set."

"I like to invite all my new hands up to a formal meal, sort of seal our deal, so to speak. Nothing like starting a business venture off on the best foot, eh?"

"Can't disagree with that."

"Good thing, too," said Mulletson. "Not a sign of promise if a man begins by disagreeing with his new boss, eh? Come, come, have a seat. I hope you don't mind, but I took the prerogative of seating you here, catty-corner from my seat at the head of the table. Figured we'd just have to shout if you were at the formal other end, eh?"

"Whatever you say, Colonel."

"Nice, nice. So," he said when they'd seated themselves, the butler helping each of them ease his chair in. "Something tells me you are a Southern man, am I correct?"

Slocum's innate sixth sense warned him of anyone finding out anything about him beyond what he cared to share. It tingled in the back of his brain like a small headache that wanted to be a big one.

"Now, sir, I make it a rule to never discuss my past, or my future, with any man." Slocum said it with a smile, something he found that usually helped ease the blow of any less-than-kind comment.

"Very well, very well. I respect a man who has personal parameters." The butler poured wine for them, and the colonel said, "But I'll take your comment as a yes. In fact, I'll wager a bit more and say you are from . . ." The little pudgy man shot a finger outward as if he were accusing Slocum of stealing silver. "Georgia!"

Slocum kept his eyebrows from rising, but the little man was starting to tick him off. Enough with the digging already. Maybe Mulletson had been acquainted with the old judge that Slocum killed. Then again, maybe not. The evening would tell—he was sure of it.

Instead of reacting, he just smiled and sipped the wine, a dark red with a fall-apple bite to it. "Good wine, Colonel."

"You know your grapes, do you?"

"Nope, not really. But I know what I like."

"Fine, fine. Hope you don't mind, son, but I decided to skip all the fooferaw and head right to the main course of beef and potatoes, with steaming vegetables. Okay with you?"

Slocum nodded and the man rang a little silver handbell that sat beside his silverware.

A side door opened at the far rear corner of the room, and in walked a pretty woman, no more than thirty, dark hair piled high and wearing a short black dress with white ruffles around the collar and sleeve cuffs. She held a large covered silver platter high before her face, and not until she set it down between the two men did Slocum recognize her.

It was Marybeth Meecher. Their eyes met, and for the briefest of moments, Slocum recalled everything lovely about the woman—her smile, her laugh, her well-muscled body, so strong and yet so feminine. He didn't notice much change in her face, other than the darkness beneath her eyes, as if she hadn't slept well in a long time. And the slight lines creeping outward from the corners of those eyes, like tiny feeder streams off a pretty blue lake.

She, too, paused for the briefest of moments and returned his stare. Slocum broke away, sipped his wine, and glanced at the colonel.

The man didn't conceal his annoyance at their brief exchange. "You two know one another?"

Marybeth's eyes rose in warning and Slocum said, "Naw. Just admiring a pretty plateful. You have to admit, the scent is heavenly . . ."

She lifted the silver-domed lid, revealing a platter heaped with juicy, tender-looking meat, a smaller silver bowl of boiled potatoes swimming in butter and sprinkled with parsley, and a third bowl that contained what looked to Slocum to be beets and onions tossed with something green. It didn't look all that dandy, but it smelled great.

"Well, hell," said the colonel, obviously annoyed. "Serve us up and then get back to the kitchen, dammit."

Marybeth did as he'd ordered. The colonel worked to tuck his napkin into his collar, under his paunchy chin, and said, "Lowly staff should know their place."

Slocum didn't look at the colonel, but rather at Marybeth, whose face had reddened at the remark.

"Seems to me a person who can conjure up something this heavenly smelling already knows her place."

The colonel sat there, a forkful of meat halfway to his open mouth, and stared at Slocum as if he were in denial about what he had just heard.

As she turned to leave, Slocum saw a smile on Marybeth's face.

"I am unsure if you just insulted me or not, Mr. Slocum, but I'll have you know I'm no one to trifle with."

Slocum chose to ignore the puffing up the man was giving himself. Instead he changed the subject. "Wasn't the girl I brought with me supposed to help your cook?"

"In the kitchen, yes." The fat man dunked a twist of bread into his wine.

Slocum noticed that the man couldn't seem to get the food

into his mouth fast enough. It was enough to put a body off his feed—if the feed had been anything less than this, one of Marybeth's delectable dishes.

Slocum recalled with pleasure that the woman could turn the most ordinary of ingredients into something unforgettably tasty. Slocum wondered if next the man might try dunking a forkful of the beef.

"But not with my food. I won't have anyone, well, you know . . ."

"No, I am afraid I don't."

The colonel looked at him smiling and chewing, his cheeks bunching with each bite. "No, you really don't know, do you." He set down his glass, wiped his fat, glistening lips, and said, "Well, that does beat all. You are genuinely a babe in the woods."

"Pardon me, Colonel Mulletson?"

"I am talking about people who ain't like you and me." He paused, his eyebrows rising, waiting for Slocum to catch on.

Slocum refused to make it easy for the man. He wanted to hear him say whatever it was he felt needed saying.

"Jesus H., you really don't follow me, do you? I'm talking about non-white-skinned folk. You get me now? The girl you brought, fine for obvious things, and even useful in the kitchen, but it would turn my stomach six ways from Sunday if it was that little hussy handling my food, the very vittles that go into my body."

That would take a whole lot of handling, thought Slocum. He nodded. "I get what you are saying. I don't know as I agree, but I understand you now."

The two men finished their meals in near silence, save for the colonel's steady volley of slurping and grunting and Slocum's attempts to not break into a laugh. Finally, when the last of the food had been cleared from the tray, the colonel said, "Why don't we call it a meal and retire to my library so that we might talk important business?"

"That sounds good," said Slocum. "I do have a few things I'd like to ask you about."

"Good, good." They made their way out of the dining

room, Slocum following the little fat man, who broke wind much of the way down the corridor to the library. He waddled immediately to a sideboard lined with an array of cut-crystal decanters.

"Mr. Slocum, what will you have?"

"If it's preference doing the talking, I'll take a bourbon."

"Good man," said his florid host. He poured a generous helping—too generous, thought Slocum. I'll have to watch my step with this snake.

Then the colonel said, "Would I be correct in assuming you're a man who can appreciate a fine cigar?"

"I've been known to indulge in a fine blend when the opportunity arises."

Again the colonel raised his eyebrows in apparent glee at what he'd found before him. "My word, man, most of these thugs I've been forced to hire don't know their asses from seat cushions. A cultured man such as yourself on my staff will be a balm and relief to our little outfit."

"To be honest, Colonel, there are a few things I've already seen here at the Triple T that give me pause, as the educated men say."

"Oh, and what might they be, boy? Come, come now, you can tell me. Maybe we can prevent a misunderstanding or two . . . And while I am at it, I tell you what—I am sorry you had to witness me disciplining my help. But I will tell you that in all my days as a world traveler, it pays mighty to keep lowly hirelings in their place. You understand, I'm sure, Mr. Slocum." His stare was almost convincing. Almost . . . .

Slocum sipped his whiskey, then set it down carefully. "Pardon me, sir, but if I'm not mistaken, aren't I a hired man, too?"

"Well, it's not quite like that. You are, after all, a Southern man, and an experienced wrangler, something we are in short supply of. The Mexicans and Indians, well, they hardly count now, do they? But back to your questions. Fire away, my boy," said the man as he proffered his desktop humidor.

Slocum smelled the rich, aged-wood tang of the tobacco rise up to tickle and tempt his nostrils. Be mighty easy to overlook the fact that this man was a slaver and employer of foul killers, given all these fancies. And that's just what he wants me to do.

"Thank you for the cigar—smells fine. What I'm curious about is how, for such a big spread—and there isn't a saddle bum from here to California who hasn't heard of the Triple T Ranch—why haven't I seen much in the way of cattle?"

He leaned closer to the still smiling boss man. "Unless you have some secret way of fattening half the number of beeves to twice their normal size . . ." Slocum smiled to show he was joshing the man.

Something in Mulletson's eyes told Slocum he was probing a tender spot. Getting too close to guessing the truth of the place, whatever it was that made it tick. Best let the man tell me in his own sweet time.

Then the colonel's smile dropped. "Mr. Slocum." He paused and his cigar stopped puffing like a locomotive on a steep grade. "I have a certain sense about people. Call it a gift, if you will, but it has never let me down. In all my years as a businessman—lumber in the Northwest Territories, ice and coal on the schooner trade back in old New England, cotton storage and shipping in the Deep South—in all my years as a businessman, I have never been let down by what I call my seventh sense. I employ it as a way of estimating the type of person I'm dealing with. And, Mr. Slocum, I can tell you are . . ."

With the speed of a striking diamondback, the colonel's pink hand shot outward and his smile reappeared. ". . . a most trustworthy and perceptive man. And those are qualities I value highly. Marry those with a vital third quality, that of being tight-lipped—I believe they call it 'riding for the brand' out here—and not only will that employee be highly valued, he will be richly rewarded."

The man held the hand out before him, waiting for Slocum to shake it. Time for the dog-and-pony show, ladies and gents, thought Slocum. He pasted on a pie-eating grin and bobbed his head while he shook the man's hand. "Just so happens, Colonel, that those three qualities are my best ones—and ones that I have in spades. Looks like we were meant to meet, if you know what I mean."

"Good, good. More bourbon?"

"No, no, not just yet. It's of such a fine quality that I hate to rush the experience. I will say, though, that you are a hand at speechifying, sir. Pure pearls of pretty wisdom haven't flowed like that since Daniel Webster was in his prime."

The ranch owner puffed himself up, thumbed the lapels on his velvet smoking jacket, and rocked back on his heels, liking what he was hearing.

All this amused Slocum, but he wasn't really getting any answers. If he could just track down Marybeth, he might be able to figure out a next step. First he had to get out of this man's study. If the man was as obtuse as he seemed, and Slocum didn't think for one minute that he really was—then he seemed lonely and wanted a drinking buddy. Not tonight—or any night with the likes of you, thought Slocum.

"So, Colonel, if I have passed your character test, is there anything that I should know before I head back to the bunkhouse and join the men for tomorrow? I'd guess, given the time of year and all, that we'll be gathering for a drive. Moving young stock to higher feed, that sort of thing."

"You really are a worker, aren't you, Mr. Slocum?"

A hard, quick knock from behind them caused both men to look toward the heavy mahogany doors. "Come in," said Mulletson.

The wizened butler stepped into the room. "Begging your pardon, sir, but I have cause to discuss a small, private matter with you."

Slocum watched the fat man's face, caught a slight rise in the eyebrows, then a nod.

"Very well, Pervis," said the colonel.

"I should be taking my leave anyway, Colonel. Busy day tomorrow."

But his host had already sailed across the room to the entryway and had engaged in a low flurry of whispers. All Slocum could make out was when the colonel said, "Oh, he does, does he? We'll see . . ." Then he inclined his eyes and saw Slocum watching him. The colonel smiled. "Well, that will be all for now. Thank you for the update. Please keep me informed."

The butler left soundlessly and Mulletson strode back to his guest. He clapped a hand on Slocum's shoulder and steered him toward the door. "Time enough for explanation of that sort tomorrow. But as you say, it's nighttime now and there is lots to do come sunup. I trust you can find your way to the bunkhouse?"

"You bet." Slocum felt himself getting the bum's rush in what had become an interesting turn of events. Not one he expected, given the way this character had been acting, but he could've touched a nerve again. Might as well make the most of it while I'm here, he thought.

Slocum indulged in a theatrical yawn-and-stretch. "You'll pardon me, but it has been a long day in the saddle. All those headaches and whatnot."

The man nodded, smiled, and at the door of his library said, "Pervis will see you to the door." And with that, the tall, thin old man in the black suit stepped out of the shadows and extended a gloved hand toward the foyer.

Slocum turned to his host to try one more time. "Huh, I'd half expected that pretty cook of yours to be moseying around, helping people with doors and hats and all." He winked and failed to see any change in the man's face.

"Oh, one more thing," said Slocum, wedging a boot in the closing door. "I trust the girl, Tita, will be treated well? Seeing as how I brought her along, I feel a certain personal responsibility toward her. You understand."

"Of course," said the colonel. "And not to worry. She will bunk in with the other girl in our cook's charge, a slovenly Indian who has nearly run out her welcome in my good graces. The poor thing cannot make a bed nor start a fire to save her life. I should have known better, but dear Miss Meecher insisted that I keep the girl on as a scullery maid.

"We tried her in the kitchen but she is hopeless. Put a knife in her hand and the dull-witted thing tries to stab to death whatever is put in front of her. Slicing a potato is an opportunity for a near-beheading. The poor thing's quite deluded. But Miss Meecher insists she can remedy the foul creature, so we keep her on and pray she doesn't scalp us in our sleep."

"I see. Well, as I said, my concern is for the girl, Tita. I would take it very poorly should she come to harm."

"Why, Mr. Slocum, are you threatening me?"

"Nothing of the sort, Colonel. I merely want to let you know my position on the matter."

The little man's frosty demeanor hardened over his face once again. "And that you have done, Mr. Slocum. Good night to you."

"And likewise to you, Colonel." Slocum touched his hat brim and nodded, but the man had already turned and the door was almost shut. He walked down the broad front steps of the house, puffing his cigar and in no hurry to head back to the bunkhouse. He hadn't made any friends since arriving here, but that couldn't be helped now. Could have been prevented had these fools not acted like jackasses toward him. But again, too late to worry about.

He'd gone but a half-dozen yards, angling toward the right where the barns lay. He figured he'd check on the Appaloosa. He didn't think Harley would have gone back in that stall considering the going-over the Appy had given the boy, but with someone that dimwitted, it was difficult to predict just how he'd act.

From his right, Slocum heard a hissing sound. He paused. Then he heard it again, not a hissing, but a distinctive *"Pssst!"* of someone trying to draw attention to themselves. He stood stock-still, just in case whoever it was had been beckoning someone else. He didn't want to attract attention to himself.

"Oh, for heaven's sake," whispered a woman's voice. "I'm over here, John."

He knew the voice—it was the woman most on his mind in recent days, Marybeth Meecher.

"Over here, by the small shed."

He remained in shadow, approached the spot with caution. Just because he believed her innocent didn't mean she wasn't being forced to lure him into a trap. As soon as he drew close to the shed, he felt two arms warp around him. He tensed, then smelled a familiar lavender soap scent and knew Marybeth Meecher was back in his arms—at least for the length of a hug.

"Marybeth," he whispered. "Are you okay?"

"Yes, yes, I'm fine."

"This isn't the safest of places to talk," he said, looking into the dark around them.

"I know," she whispered. "Follow me." She took his hand and he was reminded once again of how he had missed her in the last three years, more than he cared to admit. And that they should now meet in such a bizarre fashion seemed almost funny. Almost.

"Where are we going?"

"Back to my room, just off the summer kitchen out back of the main house. We should be safe there. Now keep quiet."

Yes, ma'am, he thought, smiling in the dark. She had a saucy way about her that always appealed to him. Not afraid to tell it like it was.

"Here's the door, just here . . ."

He heard a clunking knob, slight squeaks from hinges as the door swung inward. She led him into the small space, where a light glowed low from an oil lamp. Curtains on the small room's one window were drawn tight. From the dim glow he saw a single bed, a washstand, a small table that served as a desk, and a short, three-drawer bureau. As he took in the room, he completed the circle and his eyes landed on Marybeth, looking much the same as she had serving supper.

She embraced him again, pulling his face down to meet hers. This was the sort of greeting he had only imagined along the trail that he'd find from her one day. They kissed for a long moment, as much caught up in the thin but strong trail of memories they shared as the passion rising between them. He held her shoulders, pulled her tight to him, then wrapped his arms around her.

He felt her strength even as she surrendered to his embrace. Soon she pushed her hips forward, thrusting deeply against his own. They glided together and it felt to him as if the intervening three years hadn't happened.

He hadn't been aware that she had unhitched his gun belt until he felt its familiar weight begin to slip from his waist. It clunked at his feet and her hands continued up the buttons of his shirt. He did the same with those at the back of her dress and slipped the sleeves forward until they hung loose.

She parted his shirt, ran her hands cross his chest. He felt her hot breath stuttering along his cheek, then her tongue tickling his ear. Lord, but that woman knew how to make the most of him. He felt himself rising to the occasion—and so did she, evidently, because she pressed even closer to him.

He reached down, inched her skirts upward, and felt her bare backside quiver beneath his grasping hands. He trailed his hands around to the front of her and felt the heat of her before allowing the backs of his fingers to tease and feather her. She was having none of his slow buildup, however, and thrust one of his hands between her legs as if trying to stopper a torrent. She gasped and worked him deeper, then as if remembering an earlier thought, she popped the buttoned fly of his denims apart and pushed them roughly down his hips.

Freed, his member continued its rise and was soon helped by her hot hand squeezing it and sliding along its length as if testing it for purchase. With no warning, she leapt up, encircling his waist with her legs while he laved her bare breasts with his tongue, nibbled the pebbled nipples with the tips of his teeth.

She reached down, on the outside of one leg, and grasped his member from underneath. It twitched and pulsed in her hot hands, a living, throbbing thing that she soon fitted to her entrance. Once again, without warning, she drove hard and fast at him, then on him, ramming his thickness into her as far as they were able. She paused like that, her eyes fluttered, her head lolled back, and she sighed.

The whisper of a memory scratched at Slocum's mind, and seconds before she began her next round of attentions, he knew what she was going to do—she bucked against him then, as if she were riding a green pony. It was all he could do to keep up with her and soon he felt as if he was about to lose control of the situation. So he grabbed her backside firmly and pulled her to him. She gasped at the fullness of the interruption, her face inches from his, and he strode to the bed, set her on the edge, and drove hard into her over and over.

It seemed like forever, and at the same time, no time at all had passed, and sounded to him as though she had given up on breathing. She let herself be driven into like a train throttled out and heading down a steep slope.

"Oh God, John, I can't believe . . . how good this feels." Her head lolled to the side as he slowed his pace, teasing her, sliding in and out, just long enough that he thought she might regain a little of her growly edge. And it worked.

Quick as a cat, she reached down and grasped him there, urged him with her hand to move faster, faster, until they were once again back at full operating speed. Both of them grunted and gasped until, like a far-off lightning strike marking the full power of a summer storm, they tightened together, seized in the moment as their efforts dissipated.

Marybeth let out a long, wheezing breath and stared up at him. Sweat had plastered her dark hair to her forehead. She smiled up at Slocum as he lay beside her, careful to keep their connection, even for a little while longer.

They looked at each other for a few silent minutes, then her smile faded and she turned enough to separate them, let her dress cover herself again.

He did the same with his denims, and again they were silent for a few moments. Then she turned and looked at him again.

"You never married," he said.

"No, not me. Too busy building up the business. And then the rail line went south to Dalburg and killed any chance I had of making a decent living. Now we survive by growing what we can, hunting, and tending to what few traveling strangers there are. It's a hard life, but I don't mind. Sometimes a stranger comes along who's worth getting to know."

He knew she was referring to him and his past lengthy visit. Of all his time spent on trails all over the West, it remained one of his favorite interludes.

"What's happened lately, Marybeth? What brought you here?"

She wiggled a little closer to him, put her head on his arm. Finally she spoke. "A couple of years ago, people all over the region began to disappear. My Indian friends began to tell us that their daughters and sons, young folks, old people, all were there one day, gone the next, drifting away, some of them taken in the night. They tracked them here, to this ranch. And that's where the trail grew cold. I didn't know what to think."

"But you had to do something."

"Exactly. I couldn't sit by and hear these horrible stories of people turning up missing. I showed up here pretending I was looking for work. As luck would have it, Colonel Mulletson needed a cook."

Slocum nodded. "You happen to know what happened to his previous cook?"

"No, but I can only guess she . . . vanished."

"So do you have any idea what's going on here?"

"A little, mostly from bits and pieces I've been able to pick up. But he keeps me on a pretty tight leash. Treats me well, too, though, I will say. I think he fancies me."

"Mm-hm, I happen to know he does."

She propped herself up on an elbow, smiled at him. "How do you know? Did he say something?"

"Marybeth Meecher, you aren't smitten with that nasty old colonel, are you?"

As soon as he said it, he knew he was dead wrong. Her face fell and she grew serious, concerned. "No, but he is up to something. I just haven't been able to find out all that much. As I said, he keeps a tight lid on things here—and a tight leash on me. I don't like it, but I can't get away. I've been here for a few months and I haven't learned a useful thing, and now it's like I'm a prisoner. I'm not allowed to leave. He always makes up some excuse that prevents me. At the very least I wish I knew how things were at my place."

"You mean with Miguel and Tita? But I thought she would have told you by now."

She sat up. "What? John, is she here?"

"You mean you haven't seen her?"

"No. John, what is going on?"

"I stopped by your place, and she came here with me."

"What? Why would you bring her here, of all places? And how could you get her out of Miguel's sight?"

"He's gone, Marybeth."

"What do you mean, 'gone'?"

He sighed and decided it could do no good to withhold the sad news from her. "Two of the colonel's men attacked in the night and killed him. I shot them both, but I was too late to save him."

She was silent a moment, then he saw a single tear course down her cheek. A few minutes more and she spoke to him in a clear voice. "Why bring Tita here, then?"

"Because I'd promised Miguel that I'd find you. I also felt that I needed to take care of her and I was too far along to turn back toward Minton and bring her to safety. Now I'm beginning to wonder if I did the right thing. You're sure you haven't seen her?"

"No."

"Marybeth, I have to ask—is she . . ."

"What, John?"

"Is it possible that she'd somehow be in cahoots with these folks?"

"I don't think so." Then some form of recognition passed over her face.

"Marybeth?"

"I was just thinking that in the past few months before I left, she'd been gone a lot. She's a woman now, as I bet you noticed."

He was glad it was mostly dark in the room, lest she see his unbidden blush.

"It's all right. I know she's a pretty young thing. But I had thought she was off visiting a beau. At least that's what she'd led us to believe. Now I don't know what to think. It's possible, I guess, though if he'd known, it would have broken her grandfather's heart. Poor Miguel . . ."

"You can't blame yourself for his death, Marybeth. In fact, it's a safe bet that had you been there, the colonel's men might have killed you, too, or taken you as a prisoner."

"Is that so different than the life I'm now leading?"

Slocum stared at her, marveling at this feisty woman who, given the adversities and turns her life had taken of late, was still brimming with a strange and alluring vitality. "You know,

Marybeth Meecher, despite all this, and maybe a little because of it—it's good to see you again."

"Yeah, I know what you mean. Seeing you in the dining room tonight was a very pleasant surprise. Very pleasant, indeed. And now here you are again."

"Here I am," he said. "And as I recall, you were a pretty good cook. Tonight's meal didn't do anything to change my mind."

"How was dessert?" she asked.

"I'll tell you when I've had it." He leaned in and kissed her lips.

10

Slocum stepped lightly through the door, then down the steps off the back room of the summer kitchen. He waited outside in the dark until he saw Marybeth's already dim oil lamp wink out. Good, he thought. At least one of us will get some sleep tonight. As he walked, he pondered about what sort of welcome he could expect back at the bunkhouse.

The only thing he really wanted was a flat spot to stretch out with his hat tipped over his eyes and his Colt laid across his belly. Between the surprise attacks he felt sure he'd be treated to in the night by Clew and Harley, maybe he'd get a few winks in.

Out of instinct, he stuck to the shadows as he crossed the yard toward the bunkhouse, an easy task on a night such as this when the three-quarter moon lit the yard and cast long shadows angling like fingers. Muffled voices and dull thumping sounds came to him from the dark to his right. He cat-footed in that direction and came to a lean-to off a barn. He felt along its wall until his fingertips touched a window frame.

He drew closer to the window, darkened with cloth from within, and bent low almost beneath it. He heard a familiar voice, in a low raspy whisper, saying, ". . . they tell me you refuse to work, refuse to eat, refuse to drink. What good is a man if he shuns kindnesses bestowed on him? Kindnesses that out of the bottom of my heart you have been given, such as employment, food, and shelter? This I will not stand. The others look up to you and I will not have this. I will break you, damn your hide." The voice was angry.

Slocum took another step, felt a door handle, and saw a crack of light widen as he nudged it. He paused and listened.

"I'm a free man."

"What's that you say?" said the whisperer.

"I said . . . I am . . . a free man. Won my freedom in the war."

"Yes, yes, we've all heard such fooferaw. But I am here to tell you that any more mention of such hogwash on these premises will not be tolerated."

"But—"

Slocum heard a harsh slapping sound, as if someone had been strapped with a length of harness leather, followed by a groan forced through clenched teeth.

Slocum slammed open the door and peeled his Colt's hammer back to the deadly position. "That's about enough, Colonel." He stepped into the dim ring of light to see, in the far dark corner, Colonel Mulletson bent over a man tied in a chair.

The colonel turned his jowly face to stare at the intruder.

The prisoner, a large black man, struggled against his bonds even as his head lolled from repeated blows. What looked to be blood on the man's temple glistened in the lamp's pale light. The bound man looked up at Slocum through the one eye that wasn't swollen shut. There was anger sparking in that eye.

For a brief moment the only things that moved in the room were the big man's chest rising and falling, as if he'd just run a mile, and the leather strap that swung from the colonel's pink fist.

Mulletson straightened. "Well, Mr. Slocum, I do believe you have genuinely surprised this ol' boy. Well, both of us actually." The colonel stretched his back. "You see, I was just telling my employee here that insubordination will not be tolerated. As a matter of fact, I believe I told you the same thing earlier. Now, this might just be a good time for you to, shall we say, prove your loyalty to me by laying a whuppin' of respect and gratitude upside the head of this foul darkie. You hear me?"

As he spoke, the colonel's tone grew angrier, his face reddened, and he began to jab the air as if Slocum were standing right in front of him, close enough to poke in the chest.

Slocum advanced on the strange scene, debating inside how far to play along, make it through to tomorrow, or try to pull the bung on this barrel and drain it right here and now. He glanced down at the man in the chair. Sure, there was that spark of anger, but the man had by all visible means been badly used. His clothing hung in filthy tatters, and his footwear consisted of leather husks that might have once been boots but were now puckered, curled, and held on to the man's feet by strips of ragged cloth.

Even from five feet away, Slocum could smell the unwashed stench of the man. From what he'd heard, he guessed this was one of the colonel's gold mine slaves, and a former slave to boot. It sounded to Slocum as if this man had fallen from the frying pan into the fire. Slocum lingered on the colonel's proposal a little too long, and then he saw the little fat man's eyes skirt to a spot just over Slocum's shoulder.

"Harley? What is it, boy? Don't you see we're busy here?"

"Yes sir, Colonel. Only I thought you might want to know that I seen Mr. Slocum here."

The colonel sighed. "Yes, Harley. I think we all can agree that we can see him here, don't you?"

"No, that ain't what I mean—"

"By the way, what happened to you, boy? You look as if someone has abused you with an assortment of sticks and rocks."

"Aw, I'm okay, Colonel Mulletson. Nothing time won't solve. I just come to tell you I seen Slocum here out back behind your house, talking with your lady cook."

Slocum gritted his teeth. If ever there was a young man who needed another good kick to the backside, it was Harley. The Appaloosa's lesson was a hard one, to be sure, but not a lasting one.

"Go on, Harley." The colonel swung the leather strap playfully by his side.

"Yes sir. Well, they was talking like they knew each other, then he went on in there, into the room off the kitchen there where she stays, and he was in there a right long time, Colonel, sir."

The colonel rested one hand on the tabletop beside the little oil lamp. He looked at Slocum. "As if they knew each other . . . a right long time. . . . Hmm, that certainly sounds as if the wool has been pulled over my eyes, and for a very long time. Now what would you suggest we do about that?"

Slocum groaned inside. Here's where it begins and ends, he told himself. He forced a smile, a head shake, and said, "Are you really going to believe this little dolt over me, Colonel?"

Mulletson stroked his mustache and spade beard, his brow furrowed in concentration. "Odd as it sounds, Mr. Slocum . . . yes. Yes, I believe I shall."

Behind him, Harley snorted.

"Yes," said Slocum. "I half expected you would, Colonel."

But the white-suited man wasn't listening. "Harley, go fetch the young lady in question, will you?"

"Yes sir."

Slocum watched Harley close the door snugly behind himself. When he turned back, the colonel had a two-shot derringer jammed to the bound man's head.

"Now look here, Colonel, I was just out taking a stroll after dinner and I happened to bump into her . . ."

"The same 'her' you happened to be making eyes at during supper, hmm?" Mulletson crossed his arms. "Now really, Mr. Slocum, do you think I just came down off the mountain? No, no, no, sir, such shenanigans just won't do. That's why I had all but decided after our meal that Miss Meecher would be let go from my employ."

Surprise must have been written on Slocum's face, for the colonel continued, "Oh yes, I should have realized that a tasty little number like that would have had plenty of suitors before her time here. I had hoped she would eventually come around to recognize me as more than an employer. I had dared hope she might eventually become . . . ah, but it is far too late for that now."

He smiled, jammed the pistol harder against the man's head. "Damn good cook, though. Still, I wouldn't feel too bad about it, I was you. It was her own fault. Too uppity. Don't worry about me or my kitchen none. Plenty of other girls where that one came from, am I right, Slocum?" He winked and thrust the gun harder into the black man's head.

The prisoner gritted his teeth and grunted.

"What is it you want, Colonel?" Slocum didn't ease off on the hammer, knowing that he could easily shoot Mulletson's wrist. The thing he couldn't know is if that would accidentally cause the man to trigger a round into the prisoner's head.

"Fortunately, I have other plans for that wanton hussy."

"She had nothing to do with anything, Colonel. Leave her alone."

"I don't think so, Slocum . . ."

And then he did it again, locked eyes with someone behind Slocum.

Slocum ducked as he spun, bringing the Colt up to chest height. But as fast as he was, something solid and faster drove into the right side of his head. Maybe a freight train, or an avalanche of boulders. But he didn't have much more time to ponder it, because pinpricks of light blossomed like lightning inside his skull.

As Slocum succumbed to unconsciousness, he saw the grinning, headshaking visage of the rotund ranch owner staring down at him. The man's voice, as if heard through water, was saying, "A good job of it, my girl."

Beside him, Slocum saw a dark-skinned young woman—her face looked familiar. Tita? But why was she helping the colonel? Unless he'd read her all wrong . . .

Mulletson's face drifted back into view beside the girl's. "And I had such high hopes for you, too, boy, being as you are a Southerner and all. But I guess what they say is true—every barrel has a bad apple somewhere in it. Pity, though, as you looked like such a sensible fellow. One who wanted to make a whole lot of money. I guess I'll settle for you helping *me* make a whole lot of money."

The girl and the colonel both laughed.

And then the voices faded out and Slocum knew no more.

11

The sounds of a thousand cannon in heavy fusillade brought Slocum awake. Opening his eyes, he found, was another task entirely. He finally managed the task and saw a large black man staring down at him. Slocum tried to ask who the man was. It took him two attempts. "Who are you?" he finally managed to warble.

The big black man looked down at him and shook his head. "Not like it matters now."

Slocum tried to raise a hand. He gave up when he couldn't seem to make his brain tell his arm what to do. "I'm John Slocum."

"Why'd you come here?"

"To help."

This time, the man actually laughed at him. "Now how are you going to do that all stoved in as you are and trussed up like a ham in a butcher's window?"

So that was why he couldn't raise his arms or move his legs. Slocum closed his eyes and wondered how he got himself into this kettle of fish. It was difficult to recount the previous day's events through the thudding of cannonfire volleying just behind his eyeballs. His thoughts turned to the last things he'd seen and heard before something hit him on the head. It had been Tita, that little Mexican minx. He'd seen her staring down at him, smiling, while Mulletson praised her.

He was relieved that at least the colonel hadn't told him much more about his enterprise here. He'd find that out on his own. Usually, when someone talked enough about their business, it meant they weren't planning on keeping the person they were telling it to around for long.

"So who are you?" he finally managed.

"Man, you don't give up easy, do you?"

"No, I guess not."

"Well, being as how we're both tied up, I don't see how it matters one way or t'other just who I am."

"Humor me."

The big man sighed, looked at Slocum, and shook his head again. "Elias Jones."

"Excuse me?"

"You heard me. Folks call me Eli."

"No wonder you were so reluctant to share your name."

"Hey, I'm proud of my name. Just because your plans fouled don't mean you got to be talking down about a man's given name."

"My apologies. Can we talk about something important? Like what actually is going on here? I know it's not a ranch, and I know you were being beaten for acting out of line, and I believe there's gold involved somewhere in the mix—and not a whole lot of cattle—but beyond that, I'd like some answers."

Eli sighed again. "Okay, okay. But we ain't got much time and there's a whole lot I could tell you."

"How about you start with the high points and we'll take it from there."

"Fair enough." The big man laughed, a low sound like thunder, which tapered to a cough.

"You hurt bad?" Slocum asked.

"Nah, nothing I ain't felt before. And doled out by tougher men than these."

"Anything else you can tell me about them?"

Eli's voice lowered. "I think you're about to find out."

Slocum heard the distinctive sound of a heavy, slow-moving something being pulled in their direction.

"Wait a minute—you said we don't have much time. Why? What's going to happen?"

"One of two things—we're either going to live or die."

"Good guesses," said Slocum.

Eli ignored him. "If we die, it's because they don't want the hassle of dealing with what the colonel calls 'insurgents.'"

"And if we live?"

"Then it's because they need the manpower in the mine. And we will live because they are hard up for workers."

"Do I dare ask why?"

"You don't want to know."

Slocum gave the man a hard stare.

"Okay, you *do* want to know, but I warn you, you ain't going to like it, being as how you are headed there yourself anyway."

Now it was Slocum's turn to sigh.

"Okay, okay," said Eli. "So by first light, which by my thinking will be in about an hour, the ranch goons—I believe you met Everett, Clew, and Harley—well, a couple of the three of them will be here to load us into the wagon. That contraption will take us to the Pit."

"What's the Pit?" The entire time Eli talked, Slocum had been squirming in his fetters, trying to gain enough circulation in his limbs to worm his way free. But whoever tied him had done it up right.

"The Pit is the spot where we work. Long time ago some old fool prospector discovered gold down there and now it's a full-bore mine."

"Filled with, let me guess, slaves doing the digging."

"Yeah, you're a sharp knife, all right."

Knife, thought Slocum. They must have hit me hard, or I would have remembered my boot knife before now. He tried to work his bound hands down closer to his boots, with no such luck in sight. "So they tell me. Why is it called the Pit?"

"'Cause that's what it is—a big pit with tunnels shooting off of it. But there's two problems with it: One, it's a ravine, a canyon with no way out."

"If there's a way in," said Slocum, who finally managed

to heave himself upright and leaned against the wall of the darkened room, "then there's a way out."

"It ain't that easy," said Eli. "But you'll see soon enough."

Slocum breathed deeply, trying to gather his fuzzy wits. "You mentioned two problems. What's the second?"

"Oh yeah, the Pit? It's filled with rattlesnakes."

12

For several long minutes, the two captive men heard horses stepping slow, then a steady jangling and slapping of loose chains and squeaking of wheels, as if something large and heavy was being pulled. The sound drew closer until it stopped right outside the building they were held in. They heard two mumbles, then someone jumped down—boots landed on the ground, crunched against gravel as they drew closer. The steps of a second person joined the first.

"Rise and shine, you lazy idle loafers!" A boot slammed the bottom of the door.

It punched inward, and a different voice said, "Lemme get the damn key turned in the lock first!"

A metallic scratching sounded, then the door swung inward and two hatted figures stood just outside the doorway, silhouetted against a purpling morning sky. "Look at that, two for the price of one. Now that's a special deal, that is."

The speaker, Slocum recognized was Everett, the so-called head wrangler. The other one was Clew, aka Handsome (or used to be, thought Slocum with a wry smile).

"Thumthin' funny to you, Thlocum?" said Clew, though his voice still sounded clogged in his throat, coming as it did through his still-puffed lips.

"Boys," said Slocum, nodding. "Fancy meeting you here.

Pull up some chains and a rope. Better yet, try this one on for size—right around your necks."

Clew launched himself at Slocum, delivering a quick series of snapping kicks to Slocum's leg and side. Slocum winced but took it without a sound.

"That what you came here to do, Clew?"

"Naw, that's just a bonus to me," said the puff-faced man, glaring down at Slocum.

"We're here to drag you and the big ol' slave here down to the Pit." Everett jammed a boot of his own at the floor, scuffing it and stopping just short of a kick. "I reckon he's told you all about the Pit."

"Not really," said Slocum. "Why don't you enlighten us?"

The man snorted and, with Clew's help, dragged Slocum to his feet and outside. There, Slocum saw the wagon he'd seen from a distance the day before. Up close he recognized it as an old prisoner transport wagon, the type U.S. marshals employed to ferry several prisoners at once across vast stretches, especially when they ventured into the Nations or similar areas to retrieve their quarry.

It was essentially a steel-barred prison cell on wheels, strap steel reinforced on all corners with bar stock, forged, riveted, and pinned six ways from Sunday. This one looked as if it had been fitted out with extra steel. The door at the back had been opened and its three deadbolted locks swung loose. Slocum tried to take in everything about it as they dragged him closer. Even though his head throbbed and pounded with each step they took, he knew that each detail he soaked up, no matter how small, might help him later. That habit had helped him out of more than one scrape.

"Look it over all you want, Slocum," said Everett as they lifted him off the ground and jammed him into the opening. "But you ain't bustin' out of it. Better men than you have tried."

They slammed the door and rammed home one deadbolt as they went back inside the lean-to torture shed to retrieve Elias Jones. It was then that Slocum saw what looked to be a pile of burlap sacking and rags in the far front corner of the cage. He squinted at it—was that an elbow sticking out from underneath?

It hurt like hell to drag himself forward over the unforgiving strap steel floor, but he inched closer to the rag pile. Yes, it was an elbow, and not a man's. He heard voices from inside the shed, punches and slaps and moans.

Too bad for Eli, he thought, but it buys me time to see who this is—or was.

Slocum rolled onto his shoulder and managed to make one complete roll over to get right up to the pile. He poked at it with his chin and a soft moan came from within. And a cold feeling flowered in his gut.

"Marybeth. . . . Marybeth, is that you?"

"John. . . ." a voice whispered low, trembling.

"Hold tight, Marybeth, I'll get us out of this. They're coming back."

"Doesn't matter," came a fainter whisper from beneath the rags. "They know . . ."

He'd have time later to worry about what that meant. Slocum jerked his torso upward so that he was sitting positioned such that they'd have to get by him before they got to her. It was scant protection, and too little too late, but it was all he had to offer her at the moment.

They tossed Eli into the cage. He looked like hell, but Slocum noticed that the big man also rolled with his landing to absorb the fall without too much more damage to his already battered body. The big man winked at Slocum with his one good eye and scooched himself over to the side wall.

Everett and Clew made a big production out of slamming the door twice, as if it hadn't seated well with the first slam. Then came the deadbolts, then the big padlocks with grating squawks coming from the slowly turned keys.

Everett spoke. "You know the drill, Eli. You get out of hand, we are going to stop and take a few rounds out of all of you. Just for fun. You all just ride peaceable and quiet and we won't be forced to hoist you from them chains swingin' above your heads. You got me?"

The prisoners were quiet.

"I said . . . you got me?"

Eli's voice, strong and unwavering, said, "Yes, suh."

It probably was intended to mock and taunt his captors, but it had the opposite effect.

"Now that's more like it."

Slocum saw the edges of Eli's mouth curl up in a half-smile, saw the big man's head shake slowly, side to side.

"Now let's move on out." Everett climbed up into the passenger seat beside Clew. The man cracked the lines on the backs of the two wide-backed draft beasts and the entire contraption lurched forward, the squeaking and clanking from earlier now too shrill and harsh to Slocum.

For long minutes, the ranch receded into the flat distance, then soon was lost to sight altogether.

"Eli," Slocum whispered. "How long until we get there?"

The black man eyed him for a few seconds, then shook his head, and turned to watch the monotonous landscape pass by. Something about his demeanor told Slocum that this time he should mind the man, not make a scene. He had to get to Marybeth, had to know if she was going to make it. She hadn't sounded good, and then for her to say, "They know . . ." That could mean any number of things, none of which would be good.

He finally made a show of flopping sideways when the wagon rolled over a jarring washout. "Marybeth," he said again, timing his hissing whisper with the noise of the grating steel-rimmed wheels against rock and grit.

He tried several more times, but received the same response—nothing. Ill with worry, Slocum feared the worst. He risked nudging his head into the pile of burlap. He thought he felt some sort of response, but it could well have been the jostling of the wagon.

Then the wagon slowed and Everett said, "Maybe you didn't hear me before, Slocum, when I told Eli to keep his mouth shut. Same went for you. You should have listened, because now we are going to have to stop." He nudged Clew in the upper arm. "Pull over. I aim to take a few rounds out of Eli there. Think about that next time you wanna open your mouth when you've been warned. And you will be next."

"You want to punish anyone," said Slocum, "you do that

to me. I'm the one who brought it on. Otherwise, you'd do well to keep on my good side and we'll get along just fine."

Both men in the seat up front broke out in laughter. "That's rich, coming from a man so tied up he looks like a human yarn ball." Everett shook his head, smiling. "Ah hell, might as well keep rolling. A few more minutes and we'll be there."

That brought Slocum's head around and looking forward. From what he could see, there was nothing ahead but a flat plain to all sides, not much green except where it was choked in spots with sage. He was starting to doubt Eli's description of the place as a pit. But he knew that the very look of distance and terrain in high desert country such as this could be deceiving.

He might be able to get to the back of the cage, see more from there, and somehow land a few surprise kicks. But what good would that do? No, better just to wait it out.

Then, without warning, the prison wagon slowed. Clew urged the big horses left so that they were crosswise to the worn, rutted road they'd been following, and ground to a halt. He set the footbrake and hopped down. Everett leapt down on his side and dragged a flat bar of stock steel against the cage's strapping. The racket grated loud and harsh in Slocum's ears.

The next few minutes were a repeat of the procedure they'd undertaken in loading the two men into the rolling cage. They hauled Eli out first and dumped him on the ground, where he lay without expression on his swollen, beaten features. Slocum was next, but he had wormed his way to the back of the cage and wedged his boot heels into the rough squares made by the overlapping strap steel.

"You'd better kill me now because I'm not leaving without her."

"Keep your boots on, cowboy. She's going the same place you are. You're both lucky we're taking on whites at the present time. Elsewise you'd both be decorating a ditch somewhere miles from here."

"Yes thir," said Clew. "Coyoteth'll be howling tonight for mithing thuch a fine, fine meal."

Despite their words, Slocum didn't give up easily. Everett had to clamber up into the cage and grab the chains wrapped around Slocum's boots. It took him but a moment to drag the captive out of there. They dumped Slocum next to Eli, then Everett crawled back into the cage and scooped up the bundle of rags. A woman's leg and arm slipped out as he carried her to the back of the wagon and handed her down to Clew.

"She make it?" said Everett as he leapt down.

"How do I know? I look like a doc to you?"

Marybeth Meecher chose that moment to push aside a flap of burlap sacking and thrust her head out, then spit in Clew's face. At the same time, she flailed her untied limbs and screamed. Clew dropped her and fell backward onto Slocum and Eli, who did their best to rise to their knees and pin the man before he could draw his sidearm.

Everett lunged at the woman, who had managed to scramble to her feet.

Out of the corner of his eye, Slocum verified that it was indeed Marybeth Meecher, and that she had been badly treated, with welts and ugly bruises on her arms and legs. Her dress, still aproned from her kitchen duties, had been torn in several spots, but he was relieved beyond measure to see the hellcat in her rise, lashing, scratching, and howling.

Everett had his hands full. Miss Meecher ran full bore at him, was on him in a flash, and slashed at his face with her hands. She flailed and kicked her legs until Everett seemed to wilt under her attack, defending himself from her vicious parries and thrusts, and her howling oaths of pure rage.

She worked her hand down toward his holstered pistol and nearly had it a time or two, but he managed to push her away. And that's when all hell broke loose.

The two draft animals, agitated by the unexpected ruckus behind them, stomped and lunged, tossing their heads and whinnying, and pretty soon they surged forward. The brake budged, slipped, popped free, and they were off, dragging that massive steel cage behind them. All five combatants paused at the thunderous clatter of the rolling steel contraption.

Everett ripped himself free of the crazy woman attacking him and took off after the prison wagon, howling a blue streak and shucking his pistol. He glanced back a time or two and raised the gun as if he was tempted to peel off a few shots in their direction, but by then Clew had regained his upper hand with the two bound men on the ground.

Before they could roll toward him, the distinctive sounds of rounds being levered into rifles and the hard shouts of angry men filled the air. Slocum looked up from their dusty struggle to see eight to ten men advancing on them from beyond where the wagon had come to a stop. They were all armed to the teeth—bandoliers of bullets, skinning knives sheathed at their sides, one- and double-gun sidearm rigs, and all carrying rifles and shotguns.

"Where in the hell did they come from?" he said to Eli.

"Them? Oh, they'd be the ravine's rim guards."

"You forgot to tell me about them."

"Sorry 'bout that."

"Any more surprises I should know about?" said Slocum as Clew turned on them and drew his gun.

"Yeah, this is about half of them. But don't worry—you'll get to see the others right soon."

"How nice. I'm looking forward to it."

One of the men prodded Miss Meecher in the back and said something to her. She balked and he raised his voice again. She lay down on the ground, her hands behind her back, and he tied them tight, ran a hand across her behind. Slocum wanted to kill the man right there and then. He marked the man's face in his mind and vowed some form of revenge. When . . . he had no idea.

Clew bore down on them, thumbing back the hammer. "Gonna kill you firtht, Thlocum, 'cauth I hate everything about you. You thcrewed up my face, got me all dirty rolling around on the ground, ran off the team—now Everett'll blame me for not thetting the brake!"

The man was screaming; blue veins throbbed on his temples and the skin around his mouth had grown tight as he shouted his anger at them. Slocum saw the broken teeth in his mouth, the split and bubbled lips cracking anew with the fresh blood his rage brought on.

"Clew! Back off with that damn gun before you do something that the colonel might just chuck you in the Pit for!" This came from a rifle-bearing man behind Clew.

The damaged, angry man stood above Slocum and Eli, his nostrils flexing with his breathing, his pistol's snout glaring at them as if an extension of its owner's rage.

"Clew! Back down, dammit. They ain't worth a life in the Pit, are they? Besides, you'll get your chance."

A round of agreements and confident laughs rippled through the armed men. It worked, and a grim smile spread across Clew's face. He nodded his head and said, "You bet I will." He wagged the pistol in their faces in time with his words: "You bet I will."

13

As Clew strode away from them, Slocum said to Eli, "What next?"

"You ain't seen a thing yet."

Several of the men passed their rifles to others nearby and dragged Slocum and Eli in a line beyond where the wagon had been parked. As far as Slocum could see, ahead lay more flat prairie, and a thrashing Marybeth Meecher being dragged none too gently by the man who'd prodded and groped her a few minutes before.

Slocum didn't dare shout what he thought of the man, since he knew that any undue attention to any of them at the moment would probably do more harm than good. But where was this Pit? As far as he could tell, the plain stretched for a good long way before them.

When he shifted in the grip of the men dragging him, he was able to see dead ahead. And that's when he saw the knot of yet more men clustered around a massive wooden-and-steel winching device. It bore cogs and handles meant to distribute the weight of hauling heavy loads up and down, such as those used at a mine shaft.

The men parted at their approach and revealed what looked to Slocum suspiciously like the gondola from a hot air balloon—without any colorful balloon attached. As he watched, the big basket swung slightly and he knew that it was suspended over open air.

And that was when he could see that what he'd thought was more of the same monotonous landscape was actually the rim of a hidden ravine. How deep and how wide he'd yet to determine. But he had a feeling he'd know soon enough. And all of a sudden he made a pretty good guess as to how they were getting down into the "Pit."

Marybeth must have spied it, too, because he saw her kick up more of a fuss than she already had, but the man dragging her growled something and she ceased her thrashing.

Soon all three of them were dumped together on the ground before the large wicker basket.

"John, what's this all about?"

Several of the men laughed openly at Marybeth, but most just stood there, somber looks on their faces, their weapons pointed at the three new . . . *slaves*, thought Slocum. Not at all sure he liked the sound of that word.

"Here's what's going to happen," said the man who had dragged Marybeth. "You all are going into that basket, down over the edge, and to the bottom. Once you get down there, you will follow the others across the floor of the ravine to that cave in the rock face across the way. You see it down there? Well, that's the mouth of the mother tunnel and it leads to smaller mine tunnels. Am I right, Eli?" The man winked and smiled at the big black man.

Eli nodded. "Yeah. When you're right, you're right."

"Damn straight," said the smiling guard. "Now you just do what all the others down there are doing—digging for gold ore."

Marybeth shouted, "Like hell I will. I'm no slave!"

The man laughed. "You are now, you little dragon. Before I put you in that basket, I'll untie and unchain you. Since Eli here's been through this before, he'll go in first. Remember the drill, Eli? Keep your back to me, and at the sign of the slightest swing around, you will be shot, got me?"

Eli smirked and nodded.

"I can't hear you, boy."

"Said I know the drill. And I ain't no boy, nor no slave. Maybe once, but not now."

The chatty guard poked his hat back on his head and smiled. "Eli, if you wasn't so amusing, I'd swear we'd have killed you off by now." He looked at Slocum and Marybeth. "Just ask Eli if we're serious."

"What about food and water?" said Slocum, trying to think of anything to delay the inevitable.

While he awaited an answer, he noted that all the men, the rim guards, as Eli had called them, were white. Not a Mexican, Indian, or Black among them. It was not a surprise, just more verification that the colonel was not an even-handed employer.

"Don't you worry about that. You'll get plenty to eat—as long as you send up plenty of ore, that is." Another annoying round of guffaws bubbled up from the group.

"And to drink?" said Marybeth.

"Why, little lady, you like your whiskey, do you?" It was the same man who'd dragged her, and Slocum watched as he trailed a hand up her back, rested it on her shoulder. She shrugged it off as if it had been nothing more than an irksome fly.

The men laughed again and he shouted "Enough!" and gestured with his rifle for Eli to be brought over. They did and hefted him upright. One man bent down, sliced through the ropes wrapped around Eli's ankles, then pushed him forward toward the basket. He waited there at the edge before stepping in, and thrust out his big ham-sized hands behind him. The man's Bowie knife flashed in the sun as he made quick work of Eli's wrist ropes.

The same man gave Eli another shove and the big black man, still unused to walking after having been trussed all night and into this day, tried to maintain his balance, but ended up dropping to one knee.

The entire woven structure crackled, sagged, and swung, suspended as it was over the rim of the hidden canyon they all called the Pit. He was next, and the men were rougher with him than they had been with Eli. As they manhandled the chains around his boots, chains that also trailed up to take a wrap around his wrists, Slocum wondered what Eli had done to get up and out of the Pit. Plenty of time to ask him. He hoped.

"To the basket, boy. Ain't got all day." With that, they shoved Slocum forward to the edge of the basket, toward Eli's turned back. Slocum knew the big black man would help him if he could, but they'd been warned not to turn around once they were untied.

The last thing the rim guard did was slice through the ropes around Slocum's wrists, then two guards shoved him forward, and into the basket he went. Like Eli, Slocum dropped to one knee and fought to gain his footing. Between the swaying, creaking basket and his concern for Marybeth, his nerves jangled like a stack of gold pieces in a gambler's pocket.

"You're next, sweet thing." The same prodding fool half dragged her to the basket. Slocum risked turning his head, but he heard a hammer ratchet back and the man said, "You go ahead and spin that owl head of yours right back this way. Go ahead and I will make sure that three folks still make it down to the bottom of the Pit—but only two will be alive. You got me?"

"Yep," said Slocum through gritted teeth.

Before he knew it, Marybeth Meecher was thrust into the basket, too, and despite their precarious predicament, he felt a relief at having her, if not safe, at least with him. How he could protect her, he had no idea, nor did he know just what to expect down in the Pit.

The edge of the basket was too far away for him to peer over. But he'd seen how far up they were and it surprised him that the ravine wasn't deeper. He guessed the bottom was maybe sixty feet down. He looked straight ahead and saw the opposite side of the small ravine's rim, a good three hundred feet across. To his left and right he noted that they were roughly in the middle of this side of the rim. He guessed the ends measured roughly four hundred feet apart. All told, it was not a sizable hole, as small canyons went, but apparently plenty big enough to contain a gold mine and an untold number of slaves.

Slocum noted that it was less like a ravine than a big, flat-bottomed hole in the ground, the floor of which hosted what looked like caves at the base of the rock walls. These he guessed were mine tunnel openings, though he gathered that now only the biggest, at the base of the east end of the ravine, was in use.

Slocum was pleased to note that the broad bottom of the ravine was well lit, as the afternoon sun rode high in the sky. He fancied that eons before, the little canyon may have once had a way in and out, perhaps at the now-sealed ends. Maybe a stream had run through the bottom, a verdant grassy place for wildlife, and not the stark, rocky hole it was now. And that was when he saw the inhabitants of this place, the "Pit," moving slowly toward where he suspected they would land, slow figures clad in rags.

Without warning the basket trembled and lurched, then dropped ten feet before holding, swaying and rocking, creaking and spinning slightly in midair. From behind and above, he heard rounds of rough, mannish laughter.

"Funny fellas," mumbled Marybeth.

Down, down, down they were slowly lowered. Slocum moved a half step toward the edge of the basket and looked again across at the canyon walls.

They were craggy, but seemed nearly impossible to scale up from below, sloping inward as they did all the way around. He looked down and saw they had another thirty or so feet to go before they hit bottom.

"Judging from the scarring and repairs to this basket, Eli, I assume this is how they get the ore up to the rim?"

For the first time since they were all forced into the basket, they looked at one another.

"Of all the things a man might ask at a moment like this, you ask that, John Slocum?" Marybeth Meecher stood beside him with one hand on the rail, the other clamped tightly around his forearm.

"I'm just trying to see what we're up against."

"Figured you might," said Eli. "I can answer any and all questions you got about this place. But seeing as how you two are now officially the first white-skinned slaves down here, and seeing as how it's nigh on impossible to get out, I'd say we best start from the top." He peered over the edge. "Better make that the bottom of the situation."

Slocum nodded, and risked a look up at their captors. They were all still very much up there, and he was thankful to see there were many burly hands manning the crank wheel that raised and lowered the gondola. The rest of the guards stared back at him, rifles trained downward. And with each turn of the wheel at the top, his new predicament became more serious, more ominous, and more of a challenge than he'd experienced in a long, long time.

They were nearly all the way down when Slocum pulled his two companions into the center of the basket so that they were facing each other.

"Eli, I'd like you to meet Miss Marybeth Meecher. Marybeth Meecher, this is Elias Jones."

"Pleasure, ma'am." The big man offered a slight nod with his head. "Just so you know, them rim guards ain't going to like us fraternizing like this," said Eli, his perpetual grin spread wide on his bruised face.

Marybeth said, "Oh, *pshaw*," and parted the fingers of a hand just enough to reveal a skeleton key on a length of torn rawhide thong. "From Everett's neck," she said. Her smile and raised eyebrows told Slocum she was going to be okay.

Eli cleared his throat and said, "From Clew I got three bullets and a mess of matches down my shirt—unless they slipped out one of the holes, that is." His grin matched Marybeth's, and they both looked at Slocum.

He shrugged. "I don't have much—unless you count my boot knife."

"Well, well," said Eli. "Things are looking up."

"Looking up? We could have done this back at the ranch and cooked up some sort of plan a whole lot closer to horses and guns."

"Yeah," he said, "but there was the chance they'd come down hard on the folks here, just to squeeze us. These are my people now. My place is with them. And so is yours and yours." As he said that, he looked at Marybeth and Slocum in turn.

Marybeth offered a solemn bow of her head. There wasn't much else Slocum could do but nod in agreement.

By then, the basket had reached the bottom of the ravine. And what Slocum saw shocked him more than anything he'd seen in years.

14

The basket hit the bottom with a hard clunk. "Get out now!" a voice from above shouted.

Slocum looked up to see every rifle bristling the rim of the small canyon trained down on them. It was too far for a man to jump or punch or spit, but not too far to shout and not too far to shoot. To throw? He wondered. How about a slingshot? Take one down when the others weren't looking, maybe they could get a rifle, then . . . do what with it? He'd share the idea with Eli later.

Right now, he had to take in all that he was about to be surrounded with. He followed Marybeth and Eli out of the basket. As soon as his feet touched the hard, stone ground, the basket jerked upward.

Slocum looked around. He was beginning to gain an understanding of how deep Colonel Mulletson's bigotry ran. In the full sunlight filling the ravine, he saw all too well dozens of people, mostly old women and men, plus young boys and girls, all of them thin and all of them, save for Marybeth and himself, definitely not white-skinned. Slocum saw blacks, Mexicans, and Indians, and one old man who was probably Chinese.

Some of them shuffled from the weight of manacle chains connecting their feet, the clinking of links accompanying a slow, dragging sound. They all were dressed in filthy rags, and those that had footwear were the lucky ones, he guessed, though what they wore on their feet were grimy, rag-wrapped bundles.

The closer they drew, the more pungent the tang of unwashed bodies became. Their faces were masks of hopelessness, their bodies thin and unwashed, their hair matted tangles of rope, like twists of various colors of wet yarn.

As Slocum glanced around at the small, dull-eyed crowd, he saw that a number of them bore blackened, swollen limbs, hands with puffed fingers, cheeks and foreheads raised up as if they'd been bludgeoned. Slocum had seen enough snakebites in his time to know some of the telltale signs. But this many? And to have survived without any sort of medical help? The thought both frightened and amazed him. This was a hardy band of ill-used prisoners.

Eli extended an arm outward. "My people." He smiled a hopeful smile, but his eyes looked suddenly sad and tired, as if returning here had sapped whatever little verve and strength he had gained from his brief sojourn topside.

"What do you all eat here, Eli?" Marybeth asked, a hand to her throat, another hugging her chest.

"Not much from up there, as you can imagine. But our curse is also our blessing, in a manner of speaking."

Slocum had an idea of what he was referring to. He almost hated to say it. "Snakes?"

"You bet." The big man smiled again.

"Oh, please don't tell me that." Marybeth Meecher closed her eyes and shuddered.

Slocum put an arm around her shoulders and drew her close. "Food's food."

She pulled away and narrowed her eyes at him. "Do you at least get to cook them?" she said to Eli. "If I could cook down here, I feel I might be of some use, maybe make it through this . . . somehow."

Eli's smile dropped completely. "Begging your pardon, ma'am, but there ain't no making it through nothing down here. You work, then you die. That's it, that's all." He turned to go, then said, "And not much cooking going on. We really ain't allowed cook fires, though we make them back in the tunnels."

"If you're about done with your yammerin', you all best get to work!" The voice from on high echoed down into the ravine. "If I don't see no ore piled up for the basket, steady all day, I'm liable to forget your food!"

"Oh Lord. . . ." Marybeth looked first at Eli and then Slocum. "What is going on here?"

Slocum did his best to explain the details of the story that she hadn't yet heard. By the time he'd exhausted his knowledge of it, her eyes had widened and her mouth had dropped open. It was apparent she believed him, but also wasn't sure just what to think about it all.

"This isn't what you had in mind when you set out from your roadhouse, is it?" Slocum commiserated.

"No, John. That would be an understatement. But now that we're here, what do we do?"

They had been following Eli across the base of the little canyon to what looked like a large cave. It was, in fact, that—and much more.

"That's the entrance to the tunnel where we dig," said Slocum with a wink.

"In there?" She held a hand to her throat again.

"You're going to have to stop doing that, Marybeth, if you intend to get any ore out today." He tried to make his voice sound lighthearted and mocking, but the joke fell flat.

"You sound like you have some experience with a rock hammer," Eli said to Slocum.

"A bit, mostly placer mining, but some hard rock, too. How far does this go in?"

"Some of them go back, oh, I'd say a couple hundred feet into the rock wall. And let me tell you, it's pure rock." Eli's eyebrows rose, as if he felt a peculiar pride of ownership of it.

Slocum whistled. "She shored up?"

"With what?" Eli smiled.

As if by magic, all the other slaves began slowly walking back to work, pushing steel carts, wheels squawking, on ramshackle tracks that led from the big mine entrance. Eli had said that from there, the tunnel split fingerlike into five.

From what Slocum could see, the ore they were hauling out was low-grade stuff, and he suspected it would take whole lot of it to make much money. From the looks of it, he doubted it tested out very high in quality. How on earth did the colonel think he was going to get rich—or even pay his bills—with such low-quality ore?

"Can't he just hire people to work the mine for him? Pay them a fair wage to dig his ore? I'm sure a scaffolding and some sort of rail system could be rigged to get the ore up and out of the shaft and on up out of the ravine."

"That's the way it began, sure enough, but he's a scrimy man, is Colonel Mulletson. He's also a man in deep debt. Barely keeping his head above water, as they say."

"Couldn't you wait him out? To maintain a ranch the size of the Triple T, and an appetite the size of his, he depends on the income from this ore. Maybe you could wait him out, not send any up until he caves in, has to come down here and—"

"And what, Slocum?" Eli stared at him as if he were a simp. "You don't think we've already tried that? Six, seven months back. That very thing. You know what it got us?"

A crowd was gathering now. Slocum had dug into a nervy topic, but he had to know just what had been tried and how it had failed if they were to form any sort of workable plan of escape. He shrugged and Eli continued.

"Okay, okay," said Eli. "I get that you need to figure out what all's been done, but look, we tried that. And them guards up there . . ." He flicked his good eye upward toward the rim above, where Slocum could see the armed bastards every fifty feet or so. "They come down here in force, shot into the crowd, didn't care who they killed. I took a shot myself." He lifted his shirt, and his lean but hard-muscled waist, to the side, bore a badly healed pucker of scar tissue that a bullet would surely have made. Slocum also noticed the long lion-claw lash scars that must have been laid on Eli by a whip back when he was a plantation slave. He caught Eli's eyes and knew the man had read his mind.

"I'm sorry, Eli. I didn't mean to ride point on this."

"No, truth is, we need your help. It's bad here. A thousand times worse than ol' massah's cotton farm. But somehow, I don't know just how, I got me some hope. And as my mama used to say, where there's hope, you can be sure help ain't far behind. Even if you have to make it yourself."

"Let's get to making some help for ourselves, then." Slocum extended his right arm, and the men shook hands.

Beside them, Marybeth Meecher cleared her throat and slapped her hand atop theirs. Despite the situation, the three of them laughed.

Far above, a man shouted down to them, "Hey, you three down there! You lay off with that playin' and get to work!"

The men, women, and children who had begun to creep out of their dark places in the walls of the ravine all melted back into them, shrinking and cowering as if struck. Only Slocum, Eli, and Marybeth remained, standing defiant and staring upward, each mulling over possible solutions to a big, but not impossible, problem.

But their moment of hopefulness was short-lived.

15

Something spanged the rock face near them, kicked up rock chips, and was chased within a hair's breadth by the far-off report of a rifle. The delay caused by echo was barely faster than Slocum's gun hands drawing on . . . nothing. His sidearms had been taken, and for the first time in a long time he felt exposed and powerless.

And just as he had in such rare times in the past, he immediately admonished himself, told himself no, this was not how it was going to be—he was going to stand up to these vermin, find a way to beat them at their own game, and get these people out of this hole in the ground, this living grave.

Beside him, he noticed one of the women, a bent thing of indeterminate age, looked pained and clutched at her arm. She clamped a gnarled hand on her forearm, and red blood trickled from between her knotted fingers. Slocum was about to tear off part of his shirttail when Marybeth beat him to the punch. She peeled some of her skirt and tenderly helped the old woman, but the already-weak slave looked ready to faint. Slocum steadied her while Marybeth did her best to stop the flow and bandage her wounded wing.

"Had to be the rock chips from that shot."

"They do this to us all the time," the old woman said in a

voice as firm as a twenty-year-old's. Her tone and perfect English surprised Slocum.

"What tribe are you?"

"Lakota."

"Your people . . . don't they miss you?"

"I am dead to them. I was sold by my brother to Colonel Mulletson."

"Your own brother sold you?" said Marybeth.

"Yes, yes. He wanted things from me I should not have to give him. In the end, he took them, and then he sold me. Then I was with child. For several years I was a cook and house-keeper for the colonel. But when his money troubles began, he became angry all the time."

Another shot spanged rock close by, sending rock chips winging outward. No one appeared to get cut from them. Slocum walked out into the open. Behind him, Eli said, "No, Slocum. Don't do it—only makes 'em madder at us all!"

But Slocum was beyond caring. He raised a fist skyward, toward the rim, and said, "All right, you bastards, you want to play your games, you come on down here and do that! Fight like a man, not like the bone-sucking coyotes you are!"

He stood there, hands on his hips, and watched the effect his words had on them, these armed slave guards. One of them, from that distance Slocum could not tell just who it was, spun away as Slocum's words lanced skyward. The guard's rage was evident in the way he flailed his arms. Then he turned back to the edge and brought his rifle up to bear once, twice, three times on Slocum.

Another guard nearby shouted something to him and the man finally lowered his rifle and turned away. Within seconds he turned back again and shouted down, his hands cupped to his mouth so that Slocum would be sure to hear him. "You son of a bitch! Ain't nobody talks to me like that and lives! I will see that you pay for this! You mark what I say, you will be begging me to kill you this time tomorrow!"

The man's words echoed down on them, the last of them barely reaching the slaves down below. A breeze, such as the sort that precedes a storm cloud, rolled down into the little canyon and gusted at them in a last explosive burst before dissipating. It felt as if the man's words had created the brief but forceful wind.

Slocum saw the slaves shrink back in fear and he knew that they believed the man's speech held some magical power, even if half of them didn't know what it was he had said. Slocum also knew that if he let this thing drop now, this little fit of rage he had instigated, that he would have no power with the slaves, and the captors would have more than ever. And that would not help them in the least.

It's now or never, Slocum old boy, he told himself, and once again raised his arms. "Why wait, you little fool! Come down here and I will show you what it is to be a man. You are less than half a man, standing up there with your silly gun and acting like you own this ranch!"

In truth, he had no idea what to say, he just knew that goading them into some sort of action was far better than giving in to them and becoming a weak, dissipated version of himself. If he gave in, he'd grow weaker and weaker by the day. Then if he did finally come up with a plan, he would be too weak to enact it.

"John, what are you doing?" Marybeth said, standing in front of a gathered throng of rag-wrapped slaves. She had, as was her character, already taken it on herself to become their protector. Good, he thought. At least it will give her something to keep her from becoming like them.

"I think," Eli said, eyes cut toward the rim, "that Slocum's doing something. Bad or good, I don't know, but at least it's something."

They all looked to the rim, and sure enough, the man who had been hollering a blue streak now threw his rifle to the ground, and was arguing with the other men to lower him down into the ravine. Behind him, the same man who had admonished him before was now shouting again.

Slocum could only hear snippets, but the words did not sound particularly soothing. The last thing he heard was a final threat that had some teeth: "You like to be a slave down there, too?"

And that should have done it, but it didn't. The man who Slocum had riled said, "Hell yes!" loud enough for them all to hear. There was a pause up there while the boss man stared at the hothead, as did all the other guards.

Finally the boss man relented. Slocum saw him nod, then throw up his arms as if to say, "Okay, have it your way."

The hothead all but bolted for the basket.

Behind him the boss man shouted something that caused the man to stop just before he loaded up. Hothead turned back and the boss man shouted, "Nope. You take the other way down."

"What other way?" And that was all he had time to say, because the boss man advanced on him, poked him in the gut with the barrel of his rifle, and walked him back away from the edge.

From below, they saw the man's arms raised, heard his angry shouts turn confused, then become squeals of begging—all topped off with a single rifle shot.

Seconds later the boss man walked to the rim. "See what you made me do, Slocum? That ain't going to stand well with the colonel. If I get in deep because of it, you can bet your ass I will take you with me." He pointed a long, bony arm at Slocum. "Mark what I am saying as truth, Slocum. That be all." He turned away and shouted, "Now back to work, everybody!"

Slocum turned and headed back to the mine, but as he did, his fellow slaves eyed him with what he hoped was respect. He had caused the guards to squabble and one had died because of it. He felt as though he had won some sort of victory in the slaves' eyes, made him into someone they might trust. And that would be crucial, for he might well have need of them soon. Everyone would have to do their part in whatever plan of revolt they would settle on.

Slocum also knew that, far above, the boss was not a happy man, having to kill one of his own men to prevent some of the colonel's down-home insurgency. When would someone like the colonel learn that oppression never resulted in good things for anybody?

16

"Get him as dirty as can be."

"He's already filthy."

Slocum sighed. "I know, Marybeth, but I want him to be the color of dust, the color of the bottom of this canyon, so that he will blend in when seen from above. Right?"

Slocum knelt before the boy. Were it not for the snake, he was tempted to put his hands on the lad's shoulders. "Now, Little Dog, remember our plan? It's dangerous, but you trust me, right?"

The boy nodded, his complete faith in Slocum glowing in his shining eyes. I hope to God I'm doing the right thing and not sending this kid to his death. But it's the first part in the plan and it has to work, and I can't do it myself—has to be the boy. "Okay, when the basket begins to be lowered, I need you to become part of that wall just behind where the basket lands. But hold on to that snake, don't let it go until you get to the top, right?"

The boy nodded and held up his rattlesnake, his little hand gripped hard just behind the creature's head, its mouth opening and shutting rhythmically, tiny droplets of venom pearling from its fang tips, its tongue flicking like a miniature forked whip. The serpent's body writhed around the lad's arm, its rattles working up a hair-raising sound. It seemed as if the boy had sprouted a serpent from his arm.

Slocum turned to Eli and Marybeth. "When he gets up there, he has to make sure that snake is unwrapped from his arm, then hopefully he'll be able to whip it into the face of that near guard. He'll be close to the edge, like he always is, where the three unarmed men will be working the winch. And with any extra luck that we haven't already used up, the guard will fall down here and we'll have a gun or two. And one less guard to deal with."

Behind them, the boy nodded solemnly.

The boy's mother, the Lakota woman, said, "Make sure you pretend you are a spider and get low to the ground. Be that spider and crawl out of there—very fast!"

More nodding and confidence from the boy's eyes. Slocum wished it would be that easy. The mother and son embraced briefly, the boy holding the writhing snake at arm's length, then they parted.

He heard a sniffling behind him and saw Marybeth near tears.

"He'll be fine, Marybeth," said Slocum, raising his eyebrows to let her know that crying wouldn't really give the boy confidence. And besides, Slocum felt bad enough about sending the boy to do something he ought to do himself—but he was too big to do it. Making such a treacherous journey with a writhing, angry rattlesnake clutched in one hand while hanging on for dear life with the other—oh boy.

"Oh, I know," she said. "It's just that . . . I hate to see him holding a snake. I hate snakes," she whispered.

The boy held up the writhing creature and she stepped back, hugging herself and smiling as if she'd stepped in something foul.

Slocum knew how she felt. He wasn't particularly fond of snakes himself, but damn if the things couldn't be useful at times such as this. He just hoped it didn't attack the boy before he got up there. For some reason, the kid had a way with them.

"Go for the man nearest you," Slocum said to the boy. "Deliver the snake surprise, then get out of there while they're confused. It should be near enough dark by then that you can head that way." He pointed toward the east.

The boy nodded.

"Sounds like a bad plan, but it's the best we got." Eli eyed the rim.

Near the end of the day, when there was still enough light to work the hoist, two gunshots from on high echoed across the ravine, signaling, as Eli had told Slocum, that the basket would begin its long journey down for the last load of ore.

Slocum had made sure that the load would be a light one, but in the day's waning light, the guards from the rim would not be able to tell just how light. The boy's slight weight as he clung to the basket shouldn't tip them off that anything was odd.

He'd been prepping for it and had secreted the boy in the midst of the group of slaves pushing the creaking little ore wagon over to the spot where the basket touched down. Eli's broad back would help shield the lad while he scooted toward the ravine wall and positioned himself in the shadows, snake gripped firmly in hand.

But there would be a tense few moments while Little Dog was exposed to all the rifles lining the perimeter of the rim before the basket completely lowered.

Slocum was thankful that the colonel forbade the guards from descending into the ravine themselves—mostly out of fear, if he had to guess. They'd pushed their last load of ore to the limit timewise, to buy the lad more shadows in which to secret himself. And now all was in place.

Per prior arrangement, Eli and Slocum remained by the cart while waiting for the basket. The rest of the group dragged their slow chained legs back to the mine opening, where some of them stayed. Others trudged to the little rock grottos chipped into the sides off the canyon a step or two above the floor. There they rested the few hours before the sun heralded a new day in which they'd have to continue their labors.

As the rest of the slaves shuffled off, Eli and Slocum hunched over the wagon, rough-handling hunks of ore and making a racket, clunking them against the sides of the old dented wagon. The boy stood in partial concealment beneath the big, sweating black man's shoulder, hunched low.

Slocum hoped the boy was doing his best to keep the snake's jaws from sinking into either him or Eli. The big man mumbled something to the effect that should the snake bite him, Eli's last efforts on earth would be to pound the living hell out of Slocum.

Slocum assured him that he had complete faith in the boy. Eli grunted in agreement, but Slocum could see he wasn't wholly convinced.

As the basket descended, Eli reached up to steady it, and Slocum pretended to continue shuffling ore chunks, all the while shielding the boy's shadowy location to eyes from above. A few seconds more and he would be completely hidden.

They had agreed before when hatching this plan that they would drag out the loading process as long as possible, but even if Eli feigned more exhaustion than usual, the guards weren't averse to delivering a rifle shot or two down at him. And the last thing he wanted, he'd told Slocum, was to be shot at by a bunch of white fools who might have been nipping at their whiskey allotment a little early before shift change, and whose aim might be a little off, given the effects of the popskull and the dying daylight.

Eli began whispering to the boy as he loaded the ore into the bottom of the basket. "Just be sure you get a good grip with that one free hand of yours, stick to that backside of the basket, and get your toes dug into a spot on the bottom of the basket, too. Elsewise, you'll be hanging there and will be seen sure as shootin' as they hoist this thing up."

From the shadows, the boy's small but strong voice said, "I understand, Eli."

"Good. But whatever you do, don't move around, 'cause this thing will swing without much prompting. I've seen it go all willy-nilly in a breeze. Don't know what it'll do with a snake-handling kid hangin' from it." They were silent another moment, then Eli said, "We gained as much darkness as we could, but we're near loaded now . . ."

"Okay, Little Dog," said Slocum. "Be careful and stay

away from the edge. Most of all, if you get a safe chance, run for freedom. It will be dark enough to cover you. Run like a rabbit—not in a straight line."

"I know, Mr. Slocum. I will do my best."

"I know you will. Thank you for this."

The boy sucked in a last breath and readjusted his handgrip. Slocum saw that the boy had gripped the snake so tight around the neck he was sure it was about to expire. The thing seemed to stare through the coming dark at Slocum, even as the basket began its ascent.

He shook off the fanciful vision and worked to make sure the boy still had his back to the cliff face, and for any sign from above that the guards might have detected something suspicious.

He saw the faint outline of the basket receding the farther up it was pulled, heard far-off shouts of the rim guards. None of them sounded alarmed about anything—yet. And he had a momentary picture in his mind of the snake ready to strike. Hold that thought, he told the boy's snake with his mind. And Little Dog will be sure to deliver you to someone who deserves your attention.

But that was when something happened that Slocum could have lived without: The boy's weight began to make the basket spin on the four wrist-thick ropes, which weren't enough to keep the awkwardly laden vessel stable.

Little Dog had done his best to keep his back to the cliff face, knowing that he would have one opportunity when the basket neared the top of the rim's lip to swing himself around and into the basket. Then he would fling the serpent even as he bolted up, onto the rim, and made a mad dash for the cover of the lengthening shadows.

At least that was Slocum's fondest wish for the boy. But from where he stood, far below and half-hidden in shadow himself, it looked as if the boy might be having trouble. It was hard to tell just what was going on. Even if boy failed to hurl the snake at the man, Slocum hoped the boy didn't get off balance and fall, get bitten, or get shot.

He did his best to keep such morbid thoughts out of his mind, but they were there nonetheless. And he found himself holding his breath as he watched the slowly rotating shadow of the basket, with the outlined bump on the back side of it—the shadowed bump that should not be there. If one of the guards should happen to notice it, there could be trouble before the sort of trouble they were looking for.

In the next instant, they heard a voice from across the ravine shout: "Hey! Hold up there! Somethin's going on with that basket!"

Not a sound could be heard from below in the Pit. All eyes were fixed on the shadowy mass of the slowly rotating basket. It stopped and swung in midair. The ropes creaked like the rigging on a ship.

Presently, a big, gruff voice from straight above bellowed out: "You got to be kidding me! I'm about wore out and ready for my shift change and you're over there whining? You don't like what's going on with this basket, you get your ass over here and yarn on it for a while, see how you like it."

Another pause, during which the ropes continued to creak and sing.

"Okay then. It's on your heads, is all."

"Ha!" shouted the big voice from above. "Not likely. It'll be on theirs down in the Pit should we decide to let go of this here hoist!"

This must have struck the guards as humorous. The volley of laughter reaffirmed that these men had to have been hand-picked by the colonel from the lowest of the low, sleazy characters looking for a quick buck and unbothered by a conscience. And this gave Slocum an idea: There must be a way to play these low-wage gun bums against the colonel. What if he could persuade them that their employer, Colonel Mulletson, had no money to pay them—and no intention of paying them. That would not sit well with this group of cutthroats—of that he was sure.

A few more hauls and the basket was almost to the top, nearly in position. And that was when Slocum saw the boy make his move. How he did it with one arm free and the other clutching a live and writhing rattlesnake was impressive indeed. Slocum was sure that one day the boy—should he live through this mess—would be a formidable foe or ally.

He hoped that if they ever did meet on the trail, Little Dog would be his ally.

The creaking stopped as the basket settled into its usual place at the top of the rim, in the wooden cradle that held it adjacent to the land.

For a brief flash, Slocum saw the boy's bony leg arc up and onto the rim of the basket, the leg outlined against the purpling sky. Then all was lost to his sight. It was up to the boy, then. And Slocum didn't have long to wait for the ruckus to begin.

He saw, for a sliver of a second, the armed guard who stood beside the men operating the hoist. The man had leaned forward, rifle still held crosswise across his chest in a position not of someone expecting trouble. "Hey! What in the—"

But in the next instant, trouble was exactly what he got. His ragged screams rang out first, and in another instant Slocum saw two things moving. The boy, Little Dog, jackrabbited fast to the left, eastward along the rim, then out of sight. Slocum's breath drizzled out in a whispered volley of thanks. It looked like the kid might just make it out of there and to safety somewhere.

Then just to the right of the basket and the great bulk of the hoist, Slocum saw the gunman, skylined against the lighter purpling sky at the top of the rim, whip and spin as if he were engaged in a drunken dance atop a bar. But his screams became long and high-pitched, higher than anything a man should own up to. Still, the man held on, dancing near the edge of the rim.

The whole point of this was to reduce the guns by one, and if luck was with them, to get him to drop a weapon down to them in the Pit—anything they might use, as bargaining power or firepower.

As if in cosmic response to Slocum's request for a gift from above, the man spun in place, flailing his arms. His rifle was clutched in his hand as if it were something he might use to club the writhing, striking beast still attached to him. And in the next instant, he stiffened, pitched backward, screaming, staggering to the rim. None of his fellows dared get close enough to help him, for fear that the snake would do the same to them.

The rest of the guards froze in horror. Some of them, the ones whose mothers had raised them right, thought Slocum, put hands to their mouths and seemed to recoil.

Time slowed as the man took one, two steps, his boots hit the edge, the heels caught on the craggy precipice. His arms whipped in circles, his voice ululating like the grieving widow of a war chief howling over her slain partner. But this man was howling in sheer horror as the face of hell and agony stared him down.

And then he fell, end over end, backward and screaming, hundreds of feet. His body grew larger and larger to the Pit slaves as it dropped, pinwheeling and kicking and flailing. His arms clawed at the air, this man who mere minutes before had been annoying his fellow guards. Just that morning he'd drunk the thick-brewed sludge from the tin coffeepot at the rim guards' camp but a short distance to the south.

Despite the estimable height, the man hit the bottom fast, his body slamming against the rock like a massive hand smacking hard against stone. The sickening splatter sound was exceeded in its intensity by the sight of his head, a fragile melon, an enormous hairy egg, dropped from on high, the yolk of which blew apart in a crimson spray showering outward.

Luckily, he'd still clutched his rifle tightly as he fell. When he landed, it hit his chest, flew out of his already lifeless hand, bounced a few feet in the air, and landed with a clatter nearby. The gathered slaves didn't wince, didn't recoil. If they had been in better health, Slocum was sure they would have shouted in triumph.

Slocum took their reaction as a victory, though he knew it would be short-lived and toothless if he didn't think of a follow-up act. First things first, though, and with that he darted toward the rifle, grabbed it, then approached the body. It was now a lifeless fleshy lump without structure, all rigidity gone when every bone had all but powdered with the fall.

He flopped the body over and grabbed it by the arms.

"Help me, Eli!" he said as he dragged the dead man with all haste toward the mine's entrance.

"Everybody inside, get inside!" shouted Eli as he ran to help Slocum.

"What do you want with a dead man, Slocum?"

"This is no ordinary dead man, Eli. He's a dead rim guard. And he's bound to have something useful in his pockets. Strip off everything of use, mostly these bandoliers of bullets. I hope this gun will still work. Even if it doesn't, it's still more than we have now."

"That's not saying much."

"I know it, but it's all we have going for us right now."

They dragged the dead man as far inside as possible, and Eli lit the candle in a reflector lantern.

Slocum inspected the rifle and found that it had remained in one piece. The stock had split and the barrel was scratched—nothing that would affect the gun's usefulness. The weapon might not be accurate, but Slocum could gauge such things by one or two initial shots, then adjust accordingly. Hopefully enough to persuade other guards to drop on down and join their Pit party.

"I thought you said they wouldn't allow you any fires?"

"I said no cooking fires. Don't want us to get too comfortable, just want us to be able to see well enough to get the ore out."

"What do you think is going to happen up there?" Slocum asked as he rummaged in the man's pockets. He turned up very little, save for a worn deck of cards, a smashed pocket watch that had begun life as a two-dollar timepiece anyway, and a sack of Bull Durham. He held it up to Eli. "You smoke?"

"Not a dead man's baccy, I don't."

"Well, fortunately I'm not that discriminating." He stuffed it in his shirt pocket.

"I think that we are in for a world of hurt, that's what I think is going to happen down here," said Eli. "Last time something like this happened, the colonel himself come out, stood up there, fat as ever, and told us all he was willing to let us die down here and just replace us with a new batch of slaves. 'Course, half the folks down here didn't understand a lick of what he was saying, but I did."

"That why you started negotiating with him?"

"What's that you say?" Eli straightened and looked at him across the dead man's body.

Slocum held up a hand. "Hey, I'm not judging you. I'm just saying that there had to be a reason you were up there at the ranch when I was there."

"Yeah, well, you may be right. I seen enough of you in action to know you ain't planted by them. Nor her neither." He gestured toward Marybeth.

"So what's that mean? Is there something you know that we can use as leverage to get out of here?"

Eli licked his split lip and ran a hand over his still-puffy eye.

"Come on, Eli. I have to know. If you know something that I should, then share it." He looked out the mouth of the mine entrance. "I suspect we'll be welcoming visitors before too long."

Eli sighed. "Okay then. But it's something I got to show you, not tell you. Won't make sense otherwise."

Slocum shouted to Marybeth. "I have to go with Eli into the mine—we'll be back in a few minutes. Send Paco to get us if—make that when—they start coming down. And keep everybody in here."

Marybeth nodded and went back to cutting up snake meat.

"You know, with that rifle we'll be able to pick off anyone who gets close to the edge of the rim." Eli adjusted the reflector shield on the candleholder.

"I know. But you can bet your boots that if we know it, they do, too. Still, if we keep vigilant, we'll be able to see them. We have plenty of eyes, if not guns."

"Yeah," said Eli, cupping the flame of his candle as they wound through dark, low passages, "but the more of them we shoot, the more guns we get down here."

Slocum nodded. "If they don't break on the way down, we'll be lucky."

"We got lucky once, didn't we?"

"Yeah, but how often will lightning strike at the same place?"

"Aw, Slocum, you got to have a better attitude than that if you want to work with Elias Jones."

"Okay, then, Mr. Jones, what's this big secret you have down here?"

"A few more yards, up this way." Eli bent low and stopped in front of a rock wall like all the rest of the passage had been. He held his candle close, and that's when Slocum saw it, a vein of gold as thick as his leg and running straight back beyond where the tunnel ended—he just bet on it.

"Is that what I think it is?"

"You bet your ass it is. And no, Colonel Mulletson don't know a thing about it. I was about to try to negotiate with him, use this as leverage somehow, then he started hitting me. That's when you came in."

Slocum nodded. "What about your fellow slaves?"

Eli's eyes flashed anger in the dim flickering candlelight.

"Sorry, I meant to say prisoners."

"That's more like it. You grow up as the property of another man, you fight and claw and scratch your way to legitimate freedom, you never go back. First of all, not in your mind, 'cause if you go back in your mind, you have lost the struggle, the will to live. And that fire deep inside to keep on fighting will have gone out. And Elias Jones ain't lost his fire, you hear me?"

"I hear you," Slocum smiled. "Now can we get back to the gold?"

The big man sighed. "Okay, okay. I get a little riled at times. But this gold is the key to getting us out of here. I have been trying to figure a way to use it to make it all happen. And now that you're here, I figure we can use it—and the guns—to get us on equal footing, you see?"

"I guess I do. What's your big plan, then?"

17

Over the next day and a half, Eli and Slocum managed to deliver lead to two more rim guards, though neither one fell forward. Slocum was sure the one he shot had died or would soon die. From his sixty or so feet down, it looked to him like a head wound. He didn't feel remorse in the least for taking the lives of these men. They were vicious hired killers keeping good people enslaved.

What he did feel was anger and frustration. Frustration for the fact that the man he shot hadn't pitched forward into the Pit so they could strip his corpse clean, and anger because he could feel himself weakening in body. Slocum knew from personal experience that without proper food and water, no matter what the spirit's intentions are, a man's body wilts and curls inward under harsh conditions.

It takes a balance of all vital things—food, water, work, and willpower—each to feed the other so that they might nourish a man's working mind. And a mind, Slocum knew, was the most useful tool a man had.

The man Eli shot looked to have been hit in the side, by the way he spun and clutched at himself. Slocum guessed that if the man were hit in the belly, he'd be a bleeder. If it was a gut wound, Slocum didn't envy the man. That sort of shot could linger for days, infecting all sorts of things in there. He knew it was not a wound any town doctor would give a man two cents' worth of hope for.

Though neither man dropped a weapon, Slocum and Eli had certainly sent a message to the colonel and his men. But it was apparent that the colonel was doing the same to them—the normally meager food rations had stopped altogether. Question was—who could hold out the longest?

The Pit slaves didn't take much convincing from Slocum to get them to lay off digging ore for the greedy bigot who'd enslaved them, especially since he wasn't sending food down to them.

But how long could the colonel hold out? If what Slocum suspected was true, then the man would need that constant flow of money brought in by the ore. He could ill afford to have the production from his mine come to a complete stop. How long before his guards would revolt? How long before he was in a position of having to negotiate terms with his captives? While Slocum wondered, he kept to the shadows just inside the mine entrance, waiting for a chance to pick off another guard and, thus, to stack the odds, however slightly, in their favor.

The saving grace in all this had been the unusual number of rattlesnakes living down in the Pit. It seemed to Slocum that the foul things must be feeding off each other, because he didn't see any other way they might gain their own sustenance.

It also would account for the fact that they were unusually aggressive toward the slaves. Many of the slaves had been bitten by the creatures, but curiously, their bites hadn't been fatal. Only one slave had died from a snakebite, and that had been a little girl months before Slocum arrived.

They had taken her body to the far western end of the Pit, the opposite end of where they lived and worked. And this was also what they did with the gunman who had fallen into their midst.

A stray head of beef had fallen into the Pit months before Slocum's time, too, and the slaves had set upon it with vigor. The meat fed them for more than a week, and the green hide made useful footgear, clothing, and crude vessels for them to catch dripping water from a seeping spring far inside the mine. This slight source of water proved to be a real boon, since without it a body would not survive in such difficult conditions.

The snakes, as Eli had told them when they arrived, had been both a curse and a blessing. Slocum convinced them that a fire would be useful in cooking thin strips of snake meat, but they had to be cautious because fuel was in short supply in their rocky hole.

The rest of the meat they laid out on rocks in the sunlight. It dried, puckering and curling, and became a bit more palatable than its raw counterpart. They had to set it out and retrieve it with caution, as the guards had taken to shooting at them whenever they ventured out into the open.

Finally, on the third day after the first man's drop, Slocum managed to wing another kneeling rim guard, whose rifle spun from his grasp, teetered on the ravine's edge, then dropped down to them.

After taking the shot, Slocum still kept the rifle snugged tight to his cheek because the wounded man seemed to be having trouble getting to his feet. Slocum waited, hoping someone would come to his aid. And in the next instant, one of his fellow guards low-walked to the rim, and bent to help his comrade. It proved to be a fatal error in judgment, for Slocum triggered a round that caught the man in the upper arm, then appeared to travel straight on through into his chest.

The man jerked upright as if pulled to his feet by ropes from above, and a geyser of bloody spray plumed from his mouth. By the time it rained back down, the man had toppled forward, crumpling into a long fall that brought him to a stop in a heap at the bottom of the ravine.

His rifle followed him. His bandoliers, as with the first man they'd shot, were chock-full of bullets. As a bonus, this man also wore a double-gun rig, and was armed with a fine Bowie sheath knife. And his large boots were just right for Eli's pitifully clad feet.

A good, if grim, day of hunting.

And then came the colonel.

18

"John. John Slocum, you wake up now." It was Marybeth's whispers that woke Slocum from a deeper sleep than he expected he'd get, given the rough conditions. The floor of the mine cave's entrance, relatively free of rubble, hosted most of the slaves at night.

Slocum and Marybeth had learned early on in their days as Pit slaves that, because of the cold and the snakes, folks slept in shifts. Sleep itself was a fitful affair, punctuated by the occasional sounds of steel shovels, bars, and picks thudding into the rocky floor of the cave. It seemed that the slaves, though always exhausted, had become most adept at dispatching the wriggling rattlers with their tools at night.

Slocum and Marybeth had been assured they would be protected during their slumber. Though on waking for his shift, Slocum was not a little shocked to see the sloppy pile of a half-dozen decent-sized rattlesnakes off to the side, each body hacked close to the head, the bloodied meat bulging out of the gashes in the sleek, puckered white bodies, some of which still twitched.

"For some reason, they like to come out at night, though it's cooler then," said Eli, seeing him eyeing the pile.

"Probably because they're seeking warmth from the workers' bodies." Slocum tapped Marybeth's shoulder, interrupting

132

her staring at the dead snakes that she would soon have to help render into something edible. She'd made it clear to Slocum, though to no one else, that she didn't like snakes in the least. So for her, this entire affair had taken on an extra degree of horror. One he was relieved though not surprised to learn she looked upon as a challenge and not an excuse to run screaming.

Good thing, as there was no place to run to. He was constantly reminded being in her presence just what a good-natured person she was. Kind and driven by an urge she was not even aware she possessed—an urge to be of use to others, an urge to serve those who struggled with something, be it life itself or a simple and menial task. She was not choosy, just good.

That she was also a handsome woman, strong and well muscled, without having lost a shred of her femininity, was a fine bonus for Slocum. And once they made it out of the Pit, he hoped they might well spend a good long time together.

But first, he vowed that he would save these people from the vicious fate Colonel Mulletson had in store for them.

And Eli's secret vein of discovered gold was just the thing that could tip the scales in their favor and out of the hands of the colonel and his men. He'd spent a good deal of the earlier afternoon and much of the night mulling over Eli's plan. Then he peeled off bits and pieces of the plan, added others of his own devising, until it all came up to a workable option that would either do the trick or leave them all stranded down in the hole. But he didn't think that would happen. After all, he knew that the colonel was hard up for money and his only source of revenue evident to Slocum was the mine.

Slocum turned to Eli. "How did anyone ever discover gold down here in this hole anyway? I meant to ask you earlier, but with all the commotion with the rim guards, it slipped my mind."

The big man sighed and looked down at his new boots, pleased as punch with them. "Well, seems a few years ago, back before the colonel owned the Triple T Ranch, there was an old half-assed prospector who used to roam the range hereabouts. In exchange for the chance to prospect on the ranch land—and a free meal now and again—he would lend a hand come castratin' time, spend some time back at the ranch proper doing all manner of chores the cowboys didn't want to touch. None of it bothered him much and he liked to eat, so it all worked out pretty well for him."

"I'm sensing something that wasn't entirely to his liking was about to happen to him." Marybeth crossed her arms, her head canted to the side as she listened.

"And you'd guess right, Miss Meecher. First things first: He was out here one day, as I say, a few years back, when his burro got spooked by a snake—"

"No . . . A snake? In these parts?" Slocum tried to keep a straight face, but Marybeth jabbed him in the ribs.

"You 'bout done? 'Cause I have a story to tell and you two are just poking all manner of holes in it." Eli tried to look annoyed, but he couldn't pull it off and smiled as he continued his tale. "So the burro stiff-legged it away from him. He sees it running off at full tilt, and the old man starts bellowing for her to stop. Then, with no warning, she just disappears!"

A couple of the youngest slaves—children not much more than ten—stood close by, staring up at the big man, their eyes wide and jaws dropped wider. If they had heard the story before, Slocum wouldn't have guessed it.

"So the old man stood there a minute scratching his thinker," and Eli played up the part, running a couple long fingers across his big heard as if he, too, were scratching the thought process into being.

"But it didn't help. Not one bit." He shook his head "no" and the kids followed suit.

"So the old man walks forward, closer and closer to where he saw the burro disappear. The whole time he's looking around, for a sign of something—anything—that might help explain the situation to him. But he saw nothing." Eli looked around at his growing audience. "But he did hear something . . ."

"What?" said Marybeth, unable to contain her desire to hear the rest.

"Oh, just the long, drawn-out cries and moans of a burro dying."

"How's that?" said Slocum.

"Why, that crazy ol' dumb burro had run straight off the rim up there and fell like a hairy, sad-looking stone with big ears, and dropped right to the bottom. But it didn't die."

"What did the old prospector do?"

"What could he do? Everything he needed in order to help save it was packed on the back of the dying beast. Plus, he hated to see his old friend in such pain. But there was no way he could get down there. I heard that he ran clear around this entire rim of this canyon"—Eli's big fingers pointed along the rim above—"two whole times before he finally gave up, not finding a way down there. He shouted down to his burro that he'd be back as soon as he got help. The old man was in rough shape, his burro even worse, when he headed back to the ranch.

"So, he did get help from all his cowboy friends. They raced back to the spot, most of them unaware that the little canyon was even there. And those men were amazed to see it. They were also amazed to see how many racks of bones of beasts that had done just what the burro had done—fallen in—littered the ravine floor. You can still see them all kicked off to the far corners."

"This is a great story, Eli. But it still doesn't explain how the gold was found."

"I am getting to that, Slocum, but I won't be able to if you keep on interrupting me."

The kids gave Slocum a hard stare—and so did Marybeth. He held up his hands as if someone had gotten the drop on him.

"So where was I? Oh yes, so the old prospector returned with the cowboys, and their plan was to lower someone down to the burro, see what they could see—though they all found they had to fight the old man for the position. He wouldn't take no for an answer, and so they lowered the old guy down here on a chair secured by all manner of ropes.

"But by the time he got to the burro's side, the beast was dead—had to have been for a good few hours. So he did what any sane prospector would do. After he freed his worldly possessions from his dear friend, he decided to explore the rest of the little deadly canyon. And it wasn't long before he made his discovery. After all, there was no mistaking the color—I suspect it was the earlier version of the ore-rich vein I showed to you."

Slocum nodded, knowing about where the story was going, but intrigued enough to finish it out to the end.

"So the old man found all this promise of gold, but no way to get it out. So he chipped off a hunk of this ore, then shouted to his friends, who were up top, feeling bad that there wasn't much they could do. They lowered ropes down to him and he tied all his gear on and they hoisted it up."

Marybeth put a hand to her mouth. "They didn't leave him down here, did they?" She looked to both sides of herself as if she expected to see an emaciated old prospector walk out of the shadows.

"What do you take his friends for?" said Eli, clearly miffed. "I happen to have been one of them there that day, and I can tell you that we all made damn sure the old man got up to the rim safe and sound. We even bought him a bottle and helped him with it, toasted his old dead friend, the burro, and everything."

"I'm sorry, I just got caught up in the story."

"It's okay. If you was Slocum, it'd be a different story. But you're a fine woman and I forgive you."

Slocum cleared his throat. "I'll let that one pass. So the ranch owner sent folks down here to mine it?"

Eli looked back down to his boots. "Not exactly. He just let it go, said it was too hard to get to and the old man was probably addled anyway. Despite the rich hunk of ore he brought up from down here."

"Seems like the ranch owner would have allowed the old man to continue prospecting down here."

"Yeah, but he needed all his men to work the ranch, big drive coming up and all, so there was no one to help lower him down and haul his old skinny old ass back up again. The old man tried for weeks to get someone to lower him down. He even came out here a few times on his own tryin' to figure out a way to get down here. But nothing came of it. Then he just up and went off. Last I heard he'd died somewheres, a drunk, penniless old prospector, like most of 'em seem to end up."

"So that's how you know so much about all this," said Slocum.

Eli nodded. "Like I said, I was one of the men working the ranch. Come on up here after the war, looking for good, honest work. A bunch of us stayed on here when the spread sold. I was the only black man on the crew, and once the colonel took over, he made it plain he didn't have no use for me. Case you hadn't gathered it yet, he's one of them types. Don't like anybody who don't look like him—and by that I mean white. No offense, ma'am." He pretended to doff his cap to Marybeth.

"But someone had told him about the gold, eh?"

"Yeah, that'd be me. Let slip in a moment of weakness. He was saying as how he was going to have to let some of us go, since times were tough, all that. I could tell from day one he didn't have no experience running a ranch. Brought in a bunch of men who did things for him but none of it was ranch work. Pretty soon the herd's been all but sold off, buildings aren't kept up, all that. Then he gets rabbity. So I up and told him about the potential for gold, but on condition that he'd keep me around, maybe let me oversee it or something."

Eli looked at them. "Like the man says, 'Careful what you wish for.' Now look at me. I'm running things all right." He raised a boot and winked to the kids. "All dressed up and no place to go."

"I'm not so sure about that, Elias Jones. Seems to me we have a whole lot of traveling to do yet. And unless I'm wrong—and I don't think I am . . ." Slocum held up a finger as if making a point.

"Nor are you very humble," Marybeth said with a smile.

"Then I'd say our ticket out of here just walked up." Slocum nodded toward the rim, and there, standing at the edge, hands perched on either side of his round belly, stood the unmistakable figure of Colonel Mulletson in his white suit, skylined against the early morning light.

"I'll give him this much, the man ain't too afraid of us shooting him, is he?"

"Nope," said Slocum. "Doesn't mean we can't invite him to the dance, though." He levered a round and took careful aim at the rim's edge just before the colonel's boots.

Slocum touched off the trigger and a dust cloud kicked up. The sound echoed and the fat man on the rim jumped straight into the air and high-stepped backward.

"You son of a bitch!" came the colonel's voice.

"And a very good morning to you, too, Colonel!" Slocum was smiling as he said it. To his friends, he said, "Nothing like a little exercise to start the day off right."

"What do you want?" came the voice from on high.

"I was about to ask you the same thing! Come on back to the rim, I won't shoot."

"Kiss my Confederate backside!"

"Now, now, Colonel—there are children down here. We wouldn't want them to think you were . . . a bad person now, would we?"

"I repeat myself—what is it you are looking to get out of this deal, Mr. Slocum?"

Slocum let that hang in the air, said to his friends, "At an auction, never be the first to bid. Being a colonel, you'd think he'd know that."

"You hear me?"

"Yep, just thinkin' on it."

"I'm prepared to offer favorable terms to you, Mr. Slocum."

"You seem to forget I am not alone down here."

"Ah yes, the woman, Miss Meecher. Such a pity she double-crossed me, isn't it? But of course she will be taken into consideration, too."

"Enough with the lies, Colonel! You are holding something we want and we have something you want—and very much need. Am I correct, sir?"

"You haven't got a thing I need so desperately, Slocum. Keep that in mind. You are trying my patience and I am the very man—indeed the only man on earth—who can allow you to live or take your life!"

"I doubt that very much, Mulletson."

"That's Colonel to you, Slocum!"

"I've known colonels in my day, and you, sir, are no colonel."

"What do you want, dammit!"

"I want freedom for everyone here, and in exchange, I won't kill you."

The laughter from the rim was most audible—the dozen or so guards, plus the colonel's odd high-pitched laughter, seemed to go on and on. Behind Slocum, someone sliced the head off a snake, while others began gathering up their tools, dragging them with weak arms across the stone floor, ready for another day of grueling labor in the tunnels behind him.

"Eli, please tell them not to work today."

"Even if they'd listen to me, they are so hungry that they think the colonel will give in and give them food."

"Marybeth, try to keep them safe and not too far away. I'll need all hands on deck if this plays out the way I want it to. But keep them well away from the mine entrance. I don't trust this fat Southern jackrabbit or any of his men."

"You got nothing to bargain with, Slocum! You are playing a hollow hand!"

Slocum winked at Eli and shouted, "I have a vein of pure gold down here—and a hunk for proof. It would be more than enough to save the ranch, keep the investors off your tail, and pay those men up there. Just how long are they willing to work for a man who has no money?"

This time, the pause from atop the rim was a long one, punctuated with low volleys of shouts, and then a long stretch of placating sounds from the colonel.

"Sounds like Mulletson is busy backpeddling."

And then the man did something Slocum did not expect. The colonel shouted, "Kill them all!"

For a long moment Eli, Marybeth, and Slocum all looked at one another. Had they heard what they thought they had? And then all hell broke loose. Everything from burning brands from the rim guards' campfire to head-size rocks to clods of grassy earth began raining down into the little canyon, intermingled with a volley of bullets that seemed to fill the very air around them.

"This is just a distraction!" shouted Slocum. "Keep everyone in the mine and we'll be fine. They'll run out of missiles soon enough. We still have the upper hand!"

"I wish I had your optimism, dammit!" Eli peeked out the entrance into the bright morning sky dotted with items that rained down on them and landed harmlessly nowhere near anyplace where they might cause harm. Even the bullets whistled and ricocheted harmlessly against rock.

"If they're trying to draw us out, it's not working."

"What if they try to blast us out?" Marybeth was busy helping the others keep the curious kids away from the entrance.

"He wouldn't dare," said Slocum. "Too much value down here. He needs what we have. No, this'll stop soon enough. It's just him being angry because I called him on being broke and he didn't want to look bad in front of his men."

"Too late for that," said Eli. Even as he said it, the volley of junk from on high slowed, then stopped. A last few random bullets zipped and pinged, then they, too, stopped.

"Either they ran out of things to throw or they're gathering more missiles for a fresh assault. I don't see what he hopes to gain out of it." Slocum stood by the mouth of the mine, rifle at the ready, bandoliers strapped on.

"Hey, Slocum!" It was the colonel.

Slocum nodded, expecting to hear from the man. "Yep?"

"You still have that sample of pure gold?"

"Yep!"

"Well, send her up in the basket and I'll make my considerations."

"You know my terms, Mulletson. You free all these folks and give us safe passage, no tricks, then you get your mine and all the gold in it. But you'll have to find a better way of getting it out of here. Slavery isn't legal anymore!"

After a long ten minutes that felt like forever, during which time Slocum pictured the colonel and his cronies popping a serious sweat up there under the hot morning sun, the colonel's voice rang out once again. It filled the ravine, echoing down to them. "You bring up that sample and we'll get it assayed, then we'll talk. If it's as good as you say, it shouldn't be a problem. Then I'll give in to all the demands you want."

"No sir. I know you are going broke. You are desperate to keep your mine producing. You can't afford to hire more men—hell, you can't afford to pay the ones you have now. And you can't go steal any more people to enslave because you've picked the area clean—and it was slim pickings to begin with!"

"You keep insulting me like that, and I'm liable to chuck in some dynamite, blow you all to hell and call it a good day's work."

"You won't do that and we both know it—you need this mine open. Now what's it going to be?"

Another quiet minute passed, then: "Okay, okay, dammit. You bring that rock on up here and we'll talk man to man. No games."

"Give us a few minutes, then you can lower the basket, hoist me up."

Slocum turned back to Eli and Marybeth.

"You know he ain't going to play fair, don't you?" Eli stood there before him, massive arms folded, looking perturbed.

"I know it, but I have a few trick cards up my sleeves yet. First thing's first—we need to use that hunk of ore as the cheese to set the trap. Then we'll get our rodent."

Marybeth touched his sleeve. "That's all well and good, John, just be careful that there isn't a second mouse."

"How's that?"

"You never heard that old saw? It's the second mouse that gets the cheese."

"I don't plan on seeing any mice. Just one big rat."

As the two men headed back to Eli's gold vein, the big man said, "How you going to keep him from coming down here and laying this all wide open, killing everybody down here?"

"Eli, I will do that any way I know how. In case you couldn't tell, I'm making up a lot of this as I go along. The good news is that so is the colonel. And he's desperate."

Eli grunted. "Well, in case you hadn't noticed, we're a bunch of desperate folks down here, too."

"When I get up there, I'll do my best to throw down more arms and food to you."

"How are you going to do that, Slocum? The man gets a whiff of that sort of thing and you can kiss good-bye all your fancy negotiating."

"Don't worry. I have some ideas. My biggest concern is keeping you all safe and I'll do that any way I know how. As I said, I'm making a lot of this up as we roll along. Now, chip off a hunk of that gold and let's open this ball."

In the candlelight, Slocum watched the big man run a callused hand over the rough surface of the gold-veined wall. "It sure is a pretty slice of heaven right here." He spoke in a low voice, almost to himself. "Yessir, she's something, is this gold. I think of all the things a man could do with this wonderful fine and pretty rock."

"Eli, I need that rock. *They* need that rock." Slocum pointed back toward the mouth of the mine. "Otherwise there won't be freedom for any of them. They're all depending on you. On me. We have to make this work."

"Right, okay. I was just thinkin', is all." Eli cleared his throat and pulled in a deep breath before setting to work with a cold chisel and hammer. The ringing was a satisfying sound to Slocum. Soon, Eli had succeeded in dislodging a hunk of ore roughly the size of a human skull. Slocum put out his hands, but Eli shook his head. "Nah, I'll carry her up to the entrance."

"What's the matter," said Slocum, half-joking, "don't trust me?"

From ahead of him as they moved up the dark tunnel, he heard Eli say, "Not with this."

When they got back to the entrance, Marybeth was standing guard behind a jutting edge of rock, peering up at the rim.

"Any trouble?" said Slocum.

"I saw your rat a couple of times. He's getting bolder, keeps coming over to the rim, looking down, shielding his eyes as he tries to see in here."

"No harm in looking. Just no touching," said Slocum. He lifted the last of the bandoliers of bullets from across his chest and handed them to Eli. "Trade?"

The big man looked in Slocum's eyes and what Slocum saw there was a man of mixed temperament. It seemed as if the gold he'd found had caused some sort of change in Eli. And not one that Slocum understood or liked. He reached for the ore chunk and the big man's hand reluctantly relinquished it.

Slocum quickly slid it to the opposite side of his body, held it against his waist, away from Eli's grasp. "There's not much I can offer by way of advice. You have an odd advantage in that you have enough ammo and guns now. If you place your shots carefully, you might well be able to pick them all off, one at a time. The man is running out of hired guns. And from the numbers we've seen around the rim, I bet he lost a few in the night, especially once they heard he's broke. I'd send you, Marybeth, but I have a feeling he has bad things planned for the messenger and I couldn't bear—"

"*Ssshh.*" She touched a finger to his lips. "No need to explain. My place is here. These people need me. They need *us.* So go and do whatever you have to do to buy their freedom. We'll deal with the colonel later. I have no doubt that justice will catch up with him someday."

"Somebody will," said Slocum. "Me or the law, I don't much care who first. As long as it gets done." He expected Eli to chime in with some sage words about avenging his loss of freedom, but the big man still stared at Slocum's hand wrapped tight around the gold ore.

Slocum kissed Marybeth. She returned the parting kiss with a long, tender one, touched his cheek with the back of her hand, and then turned from him, hefting the rifle. He was grateful that she was there, bad as it was for her. But he couldn't think of a better person to leave down here with all these oppressed innocents.

He nodded once to Eli, said the man's name, and as he strode out into the open floor of the ravine, he half expected to be lunged at from behind by the big man, demanding that his precious rock be returned. He'd walked a few dozen feet when that big, rumbling voice called out from behind him. "Slocum, don't waste that pretty rock. Don't sell us too cheap, you hear?"

Slocum turned back. "You have my word on it, Elias Jones." Slocum made it all the way to where the basket would land, trying not to let the pressure of what he had to do weigh on his mind. He needed a clear mind to make this work. He watched the basket slowly descend and wished they were all going to the top with him.

Marybeth touched Eli's arm and the big man looked at her briefly, then resumed watching Slocum's progress upward.

"Trust him, Eli. He's a good man. What Slocum says he'll do, he does."

"Yeah?"

"Yeah. In fact, he's the most trustworthy man I've ever met." She watched Slocum in the basket, holding the rope supports with one hand, the gold ore chunk in the other.

"Then why did he leave you?" said Eli.

She watched a moment longer before responding. "Because he was protecting me."

"Even though you both feel that way about each other?"

Marybeth looked at him, her face reddening. "What way?"

"I may be living in a hole in the ground, Miss Meecher, but I ain't no fool."

"Marybeth. Call me Marybeth. And no, I don't expect you're a fool. As far from one as I've ever known, Elias Jones."

"So what was he protecting you from?"

She watched Slocum reach the top, the basket clunk into place, then he stepped out of the basket and disappeared from their sight. "John Slocum's a wanted man."

"What's he wanted for?"

She smiled, shook her head. "That's up to him to share with you. If he wants to. But it's not my place."

"I hear you." Eli sighed. "And your word's good enough for me. If that big ol' chunk of gold don't convince the colonel to play our way, then nothing will. Now how about we fry up some rattlesnake that I will pretend tastes like chicken. Or ham. Or anything but what it is."

19

"Well, Colonel. Looks like you're caught between a hard-rock mine and a hard place." Slocum studied the man's bloated face for signs of imminent chicanery. All he saw was a greedy man rubbing his hands over the surface of the glittering rock.

"We'll see, Slocum. We'll see." He looked up, still clutching the rock. "Now, we'll be taking a ride back to the ranch. We have a few things to discuss, after all, Mr. Slocum."

"Nothing doing, Mulletson. I'm staying right here until that piece is assayed. And we'll need food and supplies for those people."

The ten or so men offered Slocum hard stares, little more. It wasn't but a day or so ago, he mused, that they were laughing at all the little fat man's jokes. Now they all looked to him as though they'd been sucking lemons in the sun. Ah, how the mighty have fallen.

The colonel snorted. "You didn't honestly think that I was going to agree to any of that, did you?"

Slocum showed no emotion on his face, just stared at the little round, white-suited man long enough to unnerve him. Then when Slocum spoke, he did so in a raised voice so that all the men within earshot would hear every word.

"What I did assume was that you would value, if not human life, then at least the fortune waiting down there for you. It's one of the biggest veins of gold I've ever seen. And my friend, Eli, and the others are now well armed, thanks to your men here—and a few that are no longer with us, sadly." Slocum pulled an exaggerated frown and looked to the ground for a few seconds of silence. "And Eli has no intention of giving up that secret vein, which would take a whole slew of men a whole lot of time to find on their own, so deep and well has that vein been hidden."

"Don't listen to him, men," the colonel said, but Slocum saw that he was licking his lips, in obvious anticipation of such riches.

Slocum walked over to the rim and pointed to the hundreds of feet of raw rock above the dark tunnel mouth far below. He noted a brief glint of sun on steel and knew he was being watched by his friends, knew they were holding their breath and counting on him to pull this off. He put that out of his mind for the present and focused on coming through for them.

"Eli's not going to give up that mine without a fight. And if it comes to that, he's not going to give it up at all. He has enough explosive down there to seal it up for a good, long time. Long enough for you to lose this ranch, for your unpaid ranch hands to turn on you, for your investors to come gunning for you. For all manner of bad things to happen to you, Colonel. How about that?"

"Men," Mulletson called out, waving a fat hand at Slocum. "Put him in the wagon. And don't be too careful about it either."

For a few moments, none of the men made a move toward Slocum, but that changed, as he knew it would, when their thought processes recognized that no matter what the truth behind Slocum's claims was, he was not their employer at the present, but the colonel was. And up until recently, they had little reason to doubt him. And wasn't he, after all, the owner of that mine down there?

Slocum steeled himself for a thrashing, but the head rim guard thrust a rifle snout into his gut. "Get on over to that wagon. Jacobs? Take that length of rope there and tie his hands behind him."

"Now boys, that won't be necessary. I have the same

general thing in mind as the colonel, which is that we all come out of this with what we want. Beyond that, I don't care what happens to you. But tying me up won't serve any purpose at all."

The man shook his head. "Talk all you want, but we're tying your hands."

As Slocum walked toward the four-person barouche, he passed a large burlap sack with what looked to be smaller sacks of meal, cloth-wrapped bacon, and tins of foods spilling out. He stopped, toed it, and the man with the rifle behind him said, "I bet you're hungry, huh?" He offered a halfhearted laugh.

Slocum casually scooped up the neck of the sack, taking care to work the spilling contents back inside, then cinching it tight in his hands.

"Hey, what are you doing?"

Slocum walked unhurriedly back toward the basket. "All part of the colonel's agreement. Don't believe me, you ask him." He just hoped they wouldn't catch on that he was lying as he strode to the top of the cliff and, without hesitation, dropped the sack down over the edge, near where the basket always landed.

"Hey! That was our food! That was meant for the guards!"

The colonel, already seated in the back of the barouche, shouted, "For God's sake, can't you people do anything right? Tie that bastard's hands, keep a gun on him, and get him over here. I have important affairs to attend to, dammit!"

They tied his hands behind his back, tighter than was necessary. He tried to flex them to gain a bit of slack, though it barely helped, and soon his fingers began to turn red and throb like a bag of bees.

"No one," said the colonel between puffs off his cigar, not taking his eyes from the raw gold in his hands, "is to touch a hair on the heads of those slaves nor go down there until I return. Is that clear?" He looked up long enough to make eye contact with the man with the gun.

"What about our food? He threw it over the edge to them damn slaves down there."

"You are lucky I don't chuck you all in, considering how

foolish you have been behaving these past few days, neglecting to feed those poor people and forcing them to shoot at you. Damn shame, but I get what I—"

Slocum smiled at the colonel's near-slip. "You get what you pay for, Colonel? Is that what you were about to say?"

"Shut up. Drive on back to the ranch. Now!"

And they were under way, with Slocum seated in the back beside the colonel, and a familiar face driving the barouche—a laughing Everett. "Boy, don't you beat all, Slocum," he said. "I never have seen the likes of you before."

"Glad you enjoyed it. You ever catch that prison wagon, Everett?"

The laughter from the front seat stopped and the thin driver said, "You keep your mouth shut, or by God, I'll shut it permanent for you."

"You'll do nothing of the sort, Everett," the colonel warned him. "Odd as it sounds, I find I have particular need of Slocum's services. And don't think I don't know what happened to the prisoner transport wagon. I heard all about that little pitiful escapade. I expected such buffoonery from some of the others. Harley, for instance, but not you. I see that I was wrong to place responsibility in your less-than-worthy hands."

"You got that all wrong, Colonel. It wasn't my—"

"I really don't care right now, Everett. Do your best to get us to the ranch in one piece . . . and not afoot."

"I don't guess you'd consider untying me, Mulletson? My hands are throbbing something awful. I'll mind my p's and q's . . ."

"Nice try, Slocum. Soon enough, though."

From the front seat, Slocum heard Everett say, "Your head'll throb something awful . . . with a bullet in it."

"That will be about enough of that, Everett," said the colonel. "You are already in the black book over that wagon escapade."

As the colonel fell back into his ore-induced trance for the rest of the trip, Slocum wondered just what the foul little man, or his hirelings, had in store for him. Whatever it was, he guessed none of them meant for him to live long enough to get back to the canyon.

20

As they wheeled up in front of the broad steps of the grand ranch house, Slocum noted that the house, which but a few days before had seemed so imposing and elegant, looked shabbier than he'd remembered. Maybe it was because he now knew the truth about Colonel Mulletson, knew that the man would be out of money sometime soon, and might well be already. How did the man keep the whole ball rolling? wondered Slocum.

The colonel climbed down from the barouche, grunting and farting as he groped with his short legs to reach the ground. He held on to the ore sample under one arm, as one might a pillow or a loaf of bread fresh from the market.

"Slocum, goddamnit, help me down here!"

Slocum stood in the back of the buggy and shrugged. "I'd like to, Colonel, but I'm all tied up at the moment."

"Aw, Everett, get your ass down here, lend a man a hand, will you?" Then the colonel managed the rest of the drop by himself. He smoothed his jacket and trousers as Everett took his time in clambering down beside him. "Hand me that pig-sticker of yours, Everett." The colonel pointed at the broad-bladed skinning knife sheathed at the tall cowboy's side.

"What?"

"The knife, I want to borrow it to cut Slocum's hands free."

"The hell you will. I'll do it."

"No you won't. 'Cause you'll cut his hands *off*. Now give it here."

The look of pure anger shining off Everett's face wasn't something Slocum liked to see, particularly when he was bound and unprotected. He wasn't sure that Everett wouldn't just pull out the knife and let his chubby employer have it right then and there—in the gut.

Finally, the cowboy relented and, in a deft, two-fingered move, slipped the knife from its sheath. It sailed upward, he caught it in his hand, and he poised it there, point angled inches from the fat man's gold watch chain, before flipping it over, pinching the blade in his fingers, and offering the handle to the colonel.

"Pretty little tricks, Everett. However, I can assure you I don't scare easily." He took the knife and nodded toward Slocum for him to turn around. As Slocum did, he saw Everett eyeing the ore, his tongue tip passing over his lips as if he were a dog eyeing a meaty leg joint.

"You best keep your eyes on your own tasks, Everett," said the colonel, handing back the knife. "You don't, you are liable to find yourself unemployed."

"Seems to me we're all about that much anyway." Everett tipped his had back. "If what Slocum says is right, that is."

The colonel sighed and headed for the house. "Slocum, get on in here. Everett, go saddle up two horses, bring 'em out here. Me and Slocum have some business to discuss. We'll be ready in about an hour."

"Why should I?" Everett canted his hips, stood as if ready to draw.

The colonel sighed again. "Because if you don't, I won't pay you a damn thin dime for anything you've done since the last time you got paid last month. Now do the job and there will be something extra in it, I assure you, you dumb bastard." He held up the heavy hunk of gold ore and wagged it as if trying to detect a rattle from within.

"You hear that, Everett? That's the sound of pure money. Probably more than you can ever imagine. Not me, however. I can imagine a whole load of money. But suffice to say it will be a good and welcome thing, yep, and it will make us all rich men if we play our cards right. But I can't do that if you are going to stand there and act like a jackass."

They left Everett at the hitch rail, a little confused but catching on to the implications of what his boss had said. By the time they entered the cool foyer of the grand house, Everett had headed to the barn.

"Now, Slocum," said the colonel with a smile, as if none of the past couple of days had happened. "What say we have ourselves a nice meal, then we can talk about what it is I'll need you to do for me."

Slocum started to speak, but the little man held up a hand. "And what I can do for you. Yes, yes, I understand the finer points of negotiations and agreements."

"I was under the impression you had lost your cook to an . . . unfortunate mining accident."

"Ah," said the colonel, cradling the rock as he walked toward the dining room. "You are a funny man, Mr. Slocum. Very funny, indeed. But as you'll see, cooks come and cooks go. One left, another one was, shall we say, dropped in my lap." The man emitted a lecherous laugh that left no mistake as to his comment's intention.

The thought made Slocum wince. Bad enough he had to see the man standing before him, but to have to picture the foul little beast naked was an entirely unpleasant notion. The colonel rang the bell at his place at the table.

Slocum's wince continued as the door to the kitchen opened and in walked Tita, looking as pretty—and as angry— as when he'd first laid eyes on her back at Marybeth's way station.

"I believe you two know each other, eh?" said the colonel.

Spite dripped from the girl's eyes like venom off the fangs of a rattler. She clattered the serving tray before the colonel and made to stomp back to the kitchen, but the colonel snatched her by the wrist and spun her around. She did not try to fight his grasp, just glared at him with her bottom jaw thrust outward.

Slocum had seen that look on her plenty before. What he hadn't seen was the extensive bruising along the side of her face. And up around her eyes. Slocum assumed they had a special working relationship that was beyond his concern at present.

"Be a dear, little Tita, and fetch a bottle of wine." He let her go.

She spun, headed for the door, and said, "There isn't any more wine left, you fat pig. You drank it all."

The colonel's face flushed, but he just stared at Slocum and raised his eyebrows. "Hm," he said. "It appears I am no longer living in the manner to which I have grown accustomed." He hefted the rock from where it sat beside his plate. "Fortunately, that minor setback will not last long."

"Did you do that to her face, Colonel?"

"Why, Slocum? Do you still have feelings for her?" The fat man stifled a snorting laugh.

"I don't like to see any woman mistreated. Anyone who would do that shows a distinct lack of . . . everything."

"Blah blah, Slocum. If you are such a goody-goody, what are you doing up out of that hole while your friends rot down there? Oh wait, let me guess. You are not in this to feather your own nest, are you? No, no, you are hoping to learn something from me that will help tip the scales in your direction in this little debacle we have going on here."

As the colonel spoke, Slocum smelled potatoes and some sort of meat—antelope, if he wasn't mistaken—wafting from under the canted dome lid on the serving platter. His stomach growled.

"Oh, beg your pardon, but I am such a poor host. Here, Slocum"—the colonel lifted the lid—"let me fill your plate with potatoes and meat, and some greens, too. Though it looks as if that useless girl has turned them brown. No matter, food is food and I am famished."

Slocum gritted his teeth and pushed his plate away. "No, thank you, Mulletson. I will not partake of this meal. I had my fill of rattlesnake earlier, and I daresay before the day's out, I will again."

The colonel's eyes narrowed, a half smile playing on his mouth. Finally he said, "Don't be so sure about that." Then he heaped his own plate full of food.

Slocum ignored the comment. "But I would like to hear what it is you have in mind this time."

"I'll make a deal with you, Slocum. I'll tell you what you'd like to know and you tell me all there is to know about that ore down there. Hm?"

Slocum ran his tongue over his teeth. "Fair enough. You first."

"Fine, fine," said the man with a dismissive wave of his pudgy pink hand. "Mind if I eat and talk, though?" And he dove into his meal. There was still plenty of food on the platter, but Slocum did his best to ignore it, though his nostrils twitched at the aromas even this poorly prepared food offered.

It seemed to him that his sense of smell, always a keen thing, had become even more acute during the past few days of privation. Then he chided himself for thinking he'd suffered any sort of hardship, especially considering all those kids and old folks, slaving away down there for this jowl-faced fool.

The slurping and grunting slowed, and the colonel dragged a cloth napkin across his wet lips. Slocum noticed that the colonel's suit, even in the dim room, looked unusually rumpled. The napkin didn't appear to have been laundered in quite some time, and the room's furnishings were looking dusty and untended.

"You see before you a former wealthy Southern gentleman, Mr. Slocum. In fact, and this may come as a shock to you, sir, but I relied heavily, before the war, that is, on the South's slave-based economy.

"If only those uppity blacks hadn't heard those lily-white do-gooders from up North yammering on and on about how wonderful it was to be free and everyone—even slaves from Africa, can you imagine!—telling them they should be allowed to run around as if they had the full rights of whites. Why, if that hadn't happened, I daresay we would not be having this conversation right now."

"Were you in the war, Mulletson?"

"Now, Slocum, that is a complex question for which I have a simple answer and a complex one."

"Simple will do."

"Then yes, I was in the war. Didn't fire a gun, if that's what you are driving at. But I did support the South in my capacity as a titan of commerce. And that, I assure you, is what made the South a nearly insurmountable force to be reckoned with."

"Nearly."

"Why, Slocum, you cut me to the quick." He shoveled in another forkful of meat, then continued talking around it as he chewed. "Did you not fight for the South?"

"I did, for Quantrill. But that's not the point here, is it? Press on with your tale of woe, Mulletson."

"Colonel, if you please."

"I don't. Now continue." Slocum's jaw muscles bunched and he felt himself two seconds from launching himself across the table and driving a fist into the fat man's meat-filled mouth. It must have showed on his face because the colonel's eyes widened, and he swallowed and continued.

"When the plantations began to fall, left, right, and center, dammit, my cotton trade went to hell. Everyone's did, but mine was the most important one, to me, you see. If the damnable slaves had just known their place, then none of this would have been necessary, the war need not have happened. But I digress . . ."

"Yes, you do. Now get on with it, Colonel."

"Well now, aren't we impatient? No matter, I will persevere in the face of your impatience." He stuffed in a wad of burnt greens and overcooked potato. His mouth pulled wide and it looked to Slocum as if he had swallowed gravel. He gulped down a goblet full of water, made a face equally distressed—evidently not pleased with the fact he had to drink water instead of wine.

"Now, after slogging through several postwar years of hard times, and more difficult transactions than you could shake a handful of sticks at, I ended up in these hinterlands, these godforsaken mountains, this vicious terrain where it snows and people are confused about the place in the world of people who are born of a lower order . . ."

Slocum put up a hand. "I already know your views on such things. Don't foul the air in this room with them anymore. Get to the ranch."

Colonel Mulletson looked disappointed that he wasn't allowed to continue his diatribe, but he nodded. "Very well, very well. As I was saying, I arrived here as sole representative of a small but select group of investors from back East—the Northeast, I might add," and he winked. "Fools with more money than sense, fools who made their fortunes off the backs of the disgraced and impoverished promised people, the people of the grand Confederacy!" He slammed a pink fist on the table. His fork rattled on his plate and nothing else moved.

Slocum sighed.

The colonel continued. "I was charged with finding a ranch worthy of raising copious amounts of beef creatures that we might then render into meat to be sold to, well, people who are hungry."

"I gathered that," said Slocum. "How long before you realized you don't know a thing about running a ranch?"

The man merely nodded, looked down at his plate. "We experienced several bad winters, it's true. Wages were in the offing, but many of the men, a number of them quite experienced, chose to leave my employ rather than accept my promissory notes."

"Smart men," said Slocum, thinking that he probably knew a few of them. "That would explain why the Triple T Ranch, once famous in wrangling circles, fell off the map, so to speak."

"Yes, yes. But then"—the colonel's eyes widened—"someone found gold. Or rather it had been found before I bought the place, but not explored nor exploited until I had the foresight to do so."

That more or less lined up with Eli's story. Except for the part about Mulletson being smart enough to pursue the notion out of anything other than personal greed and desperation.

"I bankrolled the initial forays into the canyon's deep-set mining operations." He thumbed back his lapels, and rummaged in a coat pocket.

Slocum watched the fumbling intently, and figured he had just enough time to snatch up a fork and stab the man before he drew on him. But the fat man came up with a half-smoked cigar stub. Times truly are tough, thought Slocum.

"Problem is, we ran into a bit of a money shortage after we got the thing set up. I still needed laborers, and it is such a devil of a place to get to, as you well know. Then . . ." He tapped his temple with a fat pink finger that had a bit of meat gravy drying on the end. "I got the idea, brilliant, I might add, to do my part to resurrect the glory of the Old South. I brought back into play one of the most successful and innovative labor forces the world has ever seen.

"My men, a group of white but useless cowboys who were better with guns, gambling, and drinking than with ranch work, found and collected our new labor force. And wonder of wonders, we began to see a slight profit from the promising ore sent up out of that lovely hole in the ground!

"We also had to procure slave labor because if we attracted experienced miners, the ranch would be overrun with savage prospectors. As it is, my men had to dispatch a few of them who found out about the mine, probably from the damnable assayer in Keyville, north of here.

"Why, if we hadn't, can you imagine what this place would be like? History is rife with examples of private lands being overrun once gold is discovered. And the landowner receives nothing but an early death in Northern courts of so-called justice. You recall a man named Sutter, I take it? He owned vast lands and ended up landless and penniless. A damned shame. I wouldn't be surprised if he was a good old Southern man."

"Actually, he was Swiss."

"Good Lord. Still, I bet he supported the South in the great conflict."

"And as I recall, he bilked ownership of that land from local Indians."

"*Pshaw!* They, like the blacks and Mexicans, are inferiors who yearn to be managed, to be led by their noses. They are life's pawns. The drones in the hive of life."

"And that would make you?"

The colonel smiled and narrowed his eyes. "Through with this conversation."

He stood up, but Slocum grabbed his wrist and made him sit back down. "So you made enough from that early ore to keep your investor partners off your back, eh?" Slocum watched the man smoke, wished he had a cigar, then shook the thought off as a wet dog does water. Time for cigars—and whiskey, too—later.

"Yes, you bet, my boy. As long as we were able to maintain the bills, the investors were content to see a slow return on their investment. It took fancy footwork, I can tell you, and a couple of trips to that repugnant Northern hell known as New York City. But I managed to keep them away from us. Until now."

"So, Mulletson. Now what?" Slocum stood, dragging the man with him.

The colonel lunged for the hunk of ore, scooped it off the table, leaving a long, jagged gouge in the polished wood. He didn't seem to care. "Be losing this soon enough . . ." He winked at Slocum.

"What's that mean?"

The colonel shrugged off Slocum's grip, and said, "Follow me, Mr. Slocum." And they headed to the front door. Just outside, Everett stood at the base of the steps between two horses.

"Hey," said Slocum, despite himself. "That horse looks mighty familiar." There stood Slocum's Appaloosa, who looked to be in good shape, maybe a little lean, but then again, so was Slocum.

"Yeah," said Everett. "And I took care of him, too. Not Harley."

Slocum saw that the man took pride in this, and he nodded accordingly. "I appreciate it. He's a good horse, carried me many miles."

"And he'll carry you a few more today, too," said the colonel.

"What's that mean?" said Slocum.

"That means, Mr. Slocum, that you and Everett will be transporting, with mighty goddamn care, I might add, this very lovely chunk of golden ore. You understand me, Everett? You are to take this to that rascally assayer in Keyville. And if he don't make it a spiffy turnaround, he is to expect some trouble from you. With my permission. In fact, on my orders.

I will, of course, send a letter with the rock that will explain it all to him."

Slocum folded his arms and looked at the little man next to him. "Why do you think I need to go and what makes you think I'm about to do so?"

"Because, Mr. Slocum, if you don't, bad things will happen to those heathens in the canyon. Or as the rim guards call it, the Snake Pit."

Slocum saw mild surprise on Everett's face.

The colonel smiled. "Oh yes, Everett, I know all about what you folks say and do. More, much more than you think."

"I'm not going," said Slocum.

"Yes, you are. Because if you don't, your friends will die. And I am the one who will order it."

"Something tells me you aren't about to let go of that ore sample, Mulletson." Slocum suspected how all this was going to play out and he thought to buy himself time before mounting up. He knew it was inevitable, of course. Now that the cat was out of the bag and the colonel had been informed that the mine was capable of much more than the acceptable profits of just days before, the colonel would have no reason to keep a rabble-rouser such as Slocum alive. He would want to kill him or, more to the point, have him killed, and soon. Then the colonel would give the slaves a raw ultimatum.

Slocum swung up into the saddle—his old saddle, a comfortable seat and one he was well accustomed to. He'd missed it. "One thing more, Mulletson."

"Really, Mr. Slocum, I am a busy man."

"Indulge me."

The fat man sighed. "Very well."

"Why go to the bother of having the ore assayed right now? It's obvious to anyone who's seen it that it's far and away one of the best samples seen in these parts in a long time, I'll wager."

"That's true, that's true."

"Unless . . ."

The colonel inclined his head and smiled. "Do tell me your supposition, Slocum."

"I'm guessing that you need that piece of paper to help stave off your creditors, maybe even your restless investors."

The men regarded each other for a silent moment. Beside Slocum, Everett's horse twitched a fly, blew.

The colonel smiled. "I'll go you one better, Slocum. Between you and me and Everett here . . . the investors have sent emissaries out this way to, shall we say, poke and prod my books, find out why their investments haven't yet produced fruit."

"Occurs to me, Mulletson, that if you're telling me this, you aren't concerned if I know such intimate details about your affairs. Or maybe you figure I won't be in your employ all that much longer."

"Call it what you like, Mr. Slocum. Believe what you need to, but I have gold to dig."

"And you're not waiting for the assayer's report, eh?" Slocum backed the Appaloosa from the hitching rail.

"I hardly think so, Slocum."

"Just remember, Mulletson, should anything happen to those people in the Pit, I am a man of my word. And I give you that word now: I will hunt down anybody who is responsible."

"And what then, Mr. Slocum?" The colonel seemed amused.

"That all depends on who draws first."

"Have a safe journey to Keyville, gentlemen." The colonel waved and turned back to the house.

"And the return trip?" said Slocum, urging the Appaloosa into a walk. He didn't look back toward the house, but he heard the colonel laughing.

"Oh, but you are a funny man, Mr. Slocum. A very funny man."

21

As they rode out of the yard, pointed due northwest toward Keyville, Everett was mounted on the same horse he'd ridden a few days before when Slocum arrived at the Triple T. He held back, nodded that Slocum should ride ahead of him. Slocum couldn't blame him—he'd do the same in Everett's position.

After a few quiet minutes, Slocum said over his shoulder, "So where are my buddies, Clew and Harley?"

"Oh, I ain't seen them boys in a few days. On a mission for the colonel, I expect."

"A mission, eh? Now that all sounds very secretive to me, don't you think? As if there's something going on that somebody shouldn't know?"

"I wouldn't know nothing about that sort of thing."

"Oh come on now, Everett. Something like a secret gold mine and secret slaves? And a secret fortune that a fancy Southern colonel says he's going to share with his number one, trusted confidante head wrangler, who incidentally doesn't look to me as if he's ever wrangled anything more than a silver dollar out of an old lady's handbag . . ."

"You keep talking, Slocum. That silver tongue of yours is bound to get you in a heap of trouble. Mark my words."

Slocum let it go for a few minutes, and they rode in silence.

He would have liked to enjoy the morning, and on such a morning he normally would have. It was a fine one—high, clear blue sky, dry air, the sun hot but not yet brutal. Mountains in the distance to the west, looming large and mighty, snow on the highest peaks. He loved the mountains, missed being up in them among the pines and aspen at the tree line, especially in early autumn. Nothing like a cup of strong campfire coffee, a quirly, and bacon snapping and popping in the pan while a stream cold and clear bubbled a few feet away and your horse grazed in the dappled sun of a small mountain meadow.

He sighed. That fine scene beat the hell out of being prodded by that greedy little colonel's henchman on a horse, unarmed, while Everett had three weapons that Slocum saw— a double-gun rig and a Winchester rifle in his saddle boot. Plus the Bowie knife.

Time to rile Everett some more—maybe he'd make a mistake, do something that Slocum could use against him. He didn't think he had too much longer before the man did whatever it was the colonel told him to—kill Slocum. He didn't know Everett well at all, but something told him that the man seemed the type to shoot another man in the back.

"Everett, you don't honestly think that the colonel is going to cut you in on a slice of his golden pie, do you?" Slocum slowed the Appaloosa's pace and half turned in the saddle. He used his words to rile the thin gunhand, and also to buy himself some time to sort out the situation, see if there was something he might use against him. "Think about it. You're just his errand boy. Aren't you a little old to be anybody's *boy*?"

That got to him—Everett's jaw stuck out and his eyes narrowed. "What do you mean?"

"Ah, nothing. Don't mind me." Slocum turned around, faced front, eyeing the narrowed rocky defile they were headed toward.

The trail they were following twisted downward through a low stretch flanked by sage-crowded boulders, some of them thirty feet high. A small chasm, and the perfect place to set up an ambush. He'd do it—that was how he knew it would be ideal for just such purposes. At the same time he heard the other horse's footsteps recede.

Slocum slowed the Appaloosa imperceptibly. "Hey, Everett."

A few seconds later, the man replied, but his voice sounded forced, as if shouted from far back. Slocum half smiled, didn't turn around.

"Nothing. Never mind."

He scanned left, right. Saw a cleft in between two massive boulders, big enough to just barely glide on through, both him and his horse. But what lay back there was anyone's guess. Could open up to the other side and maybe give him a shot at outrunning whoever Everett had waiting up here. Or it could be a dead end, which was exactly where he'd find himself should it work out to be that.

Just ahead on the left, something scraped—a boot on rock? The country was too low for mountain sheep, but perfect for a two-legged varmint. Or a couple of them.

"Slocum," he said to himself in a low voice. "It's now or never."

The cleft he'd seen wasn't but a few paces ahead to his right. Within seconds he'd come abreast of it and without warning he jerked the reins hard and touched his spurs to the horse's belly.

He bent low and tucked his head down, pulled his legs and elbows in. Still the rock scraped his denims and boots on either side as he shot into the opening. He held his breath, and kept his horse moving. The rocks had formed a jumbled ceiling that kept getting lower. It was cool in there and the floor was sandy, the rock sides of the passage still tight but not yet narrowing to a dead end.

Within seconds, as he had guessed, he heard harsh, clipped snags, the words of men from behind. There was a sudden edge in their voices, as if they had been surprised. And he was the one who had done the surprising, rather than the surprise they had expected to unleash on him—a deadly rain of lead from above.

He knew who those voices belonged to: Everett, Harley, and Clew. The other two must have cut a path parallel to the road, and arrived not long before Everett and Slocum. It could mean that the trip to the assayer's office was a ruse, but probably not, since all they would have had to do was tie him up and dispose of him at their leisure. Everett must have known beforehand that they'd be making the trip.

The rock passage narrowed even more. The Appaloosa nickered in frustration, unable to proceed, though Slocum could see sunlight through the man-width gap just beyond. This presented a sticky problem, but Slocum decided he might well turn it into something of use to him. He slid from the saddle, hitched up his pant leg, and slipped out his boot knife. It wasn't much of a weapon, but it was what he had, and he was grateful for it.

"*Shh*, boy, *shh* . . ." Slocum whispered, patting the nervous horse's neck. "You need to stay here. I'll be back—I hope." With that, he slipped forward, beyond the horse, crouching low and peering ahead, then upward, as the rocks that formed the ceiling angled back and away, letting in the daylight. He paused, heard boots scuffing off to his right, up above him. He lowered down, waited, just within the shadows.

For long minutes, he heard no sounds. Another shadow from above gradually inclined longer and longer on the rock beside him. He guessed just seconds before he saw the man's buckskin shirt that it was Everett. But the thin cowboy hadn't seen him . . . yet. He leaned forward more, peering down into the gap. Of course, they all three would know that Slocum hadn't emerged from the gap.

Even now, one of them was probably cautiously cat-footing on into the tunnel, but Slocum couldn't worry about him just yet. Besides, he suspected the Appaloosa, as keyed up as he was, would probably nicker at the slightest provocation, such as a stranger coming up behind him in the dark.

The shadow lengthened impossibly long above him, and just when it seemed to Slocum it couldn't stretch any more, the snout of the man's rifle poked to within a foot of Slocum, just to his left.

So the man still hadn't seen him. One twitch and Slocum knew he'd be seen. Everett would have the upper hand, too, since he had unlimited room to pivot and swing, and he had firearms. Slocum ducked low beneath it, hoping like hell that he could act fast enough to prevent Everett from squeezing the trigger—accidentally or otherwise. A ricochet in such a tight spot would probably find a home in his body, and that he could do without.

No time like the present—Slocum's right hand flashed outward, quick as a striking snake, and grabbed the rifle barrel just behind the tip. He yanked hard and fast and the man let out a quick, low oath of surprise, but didn't relinquish his hold on the rifle, so quickly had Slocum acted.

He pulled downward hard and Everett dropped into the chasm above him—wedging there upside down, his arms pinned but flailing. In the gloom, as Slocum wrested the rifle from him, Everett's face was an inch from Slocum's, but he looked confused, didn't appear to know just what had happened. Soon enough he saw Slocum, who had laid the rifle down and reared back with a hard right fist, then planted it and followed with two quick jabs to Everett's jaw and cheek.

Slocum heard something crack, but the man stayed conscious. The blows had loosened the wedged man enough that he began sliding down. With this newfound mobility, he shucked one of his six-guns and was working to bring it to bear on Slocum.

Slocum reached for the rifle, thought better of it, and grabbed the upside-down man's shirtfront, twisted him, and dragged him downward the rest of the way into the narrow defile with him. While Everett struggled to get to his feet, Slocum popped him with another blow to the temple. Still the man stayed upright, shaking off the blow.

Must have a head of pure bone, thought Slocum, shaking his hand. The man clawed at his second pistol, the first having dropped to the ground when he was pulled downward. He cleared leather with it, but stiffened, finally, as Slocum's boot knife found purchase in the man's quivering heart.

Everett sagged forward, dead or nearly there, and in a low voice Slocum said, "Sorry it had to come to that, damn you."

He slid the knife free, wiped its slicked length on the man's sleeve, and snatched up Everett's hat. Next he relieved him of the holster, retrieved the two sidearms and the rifle, and continued onward, toward the far end of the narrow, stony corridor.

He made it to the end without seeing another shadowy figure loom down at him from above. He reached the end and then there he was, Clew, standing right out in the open, rifle brought to bear and armed with a six-shooter on one hip.

"I guess that means you got Everett."

Slocum said nothing, just spent the time gauging the distance between them—about twenty yards—and calculating the least number of moves he needed to make to kill this man who intended to kill him.

"I theen him up there on the rock, poking hith rifle down in, but there wath no way I could tell him not to do that, no way to warn him."

"It was unwise of him," said Slocum.

"But you . . . you ain't gonna get by me tho easy."

"What do you have against me, Clew? Tell me that. You'd risk your neck for the colonel? He already bilked Everett out of the most valuable thing he had—his life—in exchange for hollow promises of wealth. Is that what you're after?"

"I'm after one thing and one thing only—putting a few holeth in your foul hide, Thlocum. Ever thince you come to the ranch, there'th been nothing the thame, you got uth all beat up, near ruint my face, and now you thtand there thinking you're gonna pull one on me? Not hardly . . ." Clew raised his arms as if he'd been gotten the drop on, then smiling, he dropped the rifle. It hit the dirt by his feet with a dull *thunk*.

"Don't do it, Clew. Don't make me kill you . . ."

"Ha! You can't beat me, Thlocum. I'm top thot at the ranch."

Slocum kept a watch on the man's eyes. They were fixed on him, no wavering. He hoped that meant there would be no chance the kid, Harley, could be up behind him, ready to pounce. Didn't mean the kid wasn't aiming for him from some dark corner. Lord knows he'd given the kid and this fool reason enough to hate him.

"Go ahead, Thlocum, drop your rifle and make it a fair fight!" Even as he said it, Clew's left hand dropped, slicked his gun up out of its holster, and had just cleared leather when

Slocum cranked a rifle shot into the man's gut. Clew's eyes flew wide open.

He kept raising that gun, slower than a normal man would have, but Slocum had seen plenty of men get shot making bad judgments about dying men's reaction times. He delivered another lead pill straight to Clew's middle.

Clew whipped around as if yanked and landed on his back, twitching in the sand. Slocum would have liked to make it a heart shot, quicker and less drawn-out pain for the victim, but there was no time and the distance made it impossible.

Slocum walked to him, toed away the loosely held pistol that, had Slocum been slower, could well have rendered him the victim instead. How many more times did a man such as himself have in this life? He shook his head as Clew's head flopped to the side and his chest fell, but rose no more.

As Slocum headed around the rocky knob he'd emerged from, he hoped the kid would make a better choice than his two older friends had. So far, he'd seen nothing. Maybe the kid wasn't with them? Maybe he'd come to his senses and hightailed it on out of there. No, he would have heard the hoofbeats. He didn't dare relax his vigilance yet. Just because he'd not heard the kid, had not heard the voices of three separate men, didn't mean the kid wasn't there somewhere.

He worked his way back around to the front of the rocky draw through which the trail cut, and glancing in every direction at once—or so he wished he could—Slocum slow-walked back toward the opening. Every second spent here was a wasted second. Then it occurred to him. He hadn't seen the men's horses yet.

Instead of bearing right, he broke left to explore the far side of the roadway and the boulders clustered there that might well be sheltering the horses. He might soon find out if the kid was among them. And as he skirted the rocks and got his first view of that far side, his heart fell. There were three horses but none of them was his Appaloosa. Somehow he'd hoped that his horse had been miraculously retrieved from the cavelike tunnel.

But no kid either.

"Dammit, kid. Where are you?" he said low and to himself. He got no answer.

A bead of sweat caught in the stubble of his cheek. It felt like an ant on his face. Another tickled and itched, then slid down his eye corner and stung in his eye. He wiped his eyes clear with one grimy hand, and turned back to the other side of the road. Maybe he could get his horse out of the tunnel and ride on out of there while the kid, maybe too scared to come out, stayed put.

Maybe . . . maybe? he asked himself. Slocum, that's no way to operate. Still, he worked his way back into the passage's entrance and paused just inside. He didn't hear the horse yet, but that was no surprise, since he would have probably calmed down by now standing alone in the dark, not smart enough to back out on his own.

Was there some other sound? He was probably imagining things. Slocum advanced, his boot soles grinding out small noises that he wished would not be. He paused again. The tunnel here took a curve to the left, and then a long narrow length at the end of which should be the Appaloosa.

And that was when he heard a sound that shouldn't be there. A slight rustling that stopped as soon as it started. Sounded just like cloth against something hard—denim pants on rock. The kid?

"Harley . . . I know you're there."

A long pause finally broke with a sharp metallic click, the hammer of a sidearm peeling back to the deadly position.

"Kid, don't be a fool. Everett and Clew are dead."

"You murdering bastard . . ."

It came out little more than a whisper, but Slocum was surprised it sounded even closer than the gun's click. The kid couldn't be more than ten feet away.

"Harley, look. I'm stepping into the path where you can see me. I don't want to shoot you and you don't want to shoot me. There's been enough of that today. You understand? This can all end just fine. We'll ride back to the ranch together. Have a cup of coffee, talk this thing through. Enough with the guns."

"You're a killer and killers need to be killed!"

The kid's sudden loud voice riled the Appaloosa, far back in the passage behind him.

"Was that . . . your horse?"

Slocum almost smiled. He'd almost forgotten that was the horse that Harley had mistreated—and that had then beaten the living tar out of him. The kid obviously didn't want any part of what the horse might still have in mind.

Slocum racked in a round and stepped into the rocky corridor. There was just enough diffused light shafting in from both ends to illuminate each man from behind. The kid was about a dozen feet from him, had about six feet to go before he bumped into the Appaloosa.

"Harley, drop the damn gun. This is foolish. I have too much experience with such things and you don't. What do you think is going to happen here?"

The kid's features were barely visible in the dim light. And became less so as he backed up. The horse nickered and glanced with a half-turned head toward the kid.

"Harley, don't keep walking toward that horse. He doesn't exactly like you, remember?"

"I aim to kill you, Slocum, for all the grief you caused us." The kid's voice sounded stuttery, and shook as he talked.

"Harley, enough now. Drop the damn gun and stand still." Slocum hoped his stern voice would snap some sense into the boy, break through the fog he'd wrapped himself in.

"You go to hell, Slocum!" he called out, and he raised his gun, even as he took one more step backward.

The Appaloosa lashed out so fast that Slocum had no time to defend himself by pulling the trigger on his rifle. The kid's gun went off, spanged and caromed past Slocum and out the entrance, whizzing like a bee the whole way. But he'd pulled the trigger only as a reflexive reaction when the horse's hooves slammed into him with the force of twin steam-driven sledge-hammers. One struck between his shoulder blades, the other a bit higher, catching the kid at the base of the neck, just where his shaggy hairline began.

Slocum saw the entire thing as if time had slowed, saw the kid's eyes widen, his mouth drop open, his head snap backward from the impact, then the boy's body became airborne and pitched to a rolling, tumbled mass at Slocum's feet.

"Harley! Boy, can you hear me?"

A low moan ended in a wet cough. Slocum bent low, and the boy whispered, "Turn . . . me over . . ."

Slocum knew there was little chance the kid would live, so he complied. The kid never once made a sound in pain, and Slocum realized it was probably because his body was a deadened thing, so badly had the horse hurt the boy.

Slocum sat on the rocky ground, cradled the boy's head in his lap. "Harley, you have any kin you'd like me to contact?"

"No . . . no. I . . ."

Slocum bent lower over him.

"I ain't bad . . ."

"Of course you're not, son. You're—"

But that was all the boy would ever hear. Harley's breathing came in slowing gasps, then stopped. Slocum sat there a moment with the boy, then pulled in a long, deep breath and stood. He lifted the boy, surprisingly lighter than he expected him to be, and carried him outside.

He retrieved the three horses, draped each of the three dead men across their saddles, then went around the rock pile and in through the narrow channel, came up on the Appaloosa head first. He didn't know but the horse might still be worked up enough to lash out even at him. He backed the horse on through the narrow stone tunnel and out into the bright sunshine.

The horse blinked and nickered at the other three. Slocum slipped a hand into Everett's saddlebag, retrieved the hunk of gold ore, and secured it in his own saddlebag. Then he mounted up and led the three horses back to the Triple T.

He had wanted to race back to the ranch, but there was no way he was going to leave those dead men out there to the coyotes and vultures. They might have been misguided, but he'd gotten to know them a little and he felt more of an obligation to them than he did to the other men he'd killed who worked for the colonel.

Despite their deadweight loads, the horses were still fresh enough that they made it back to the ranch in decent time.

Still, by the time he dismounted at the rail before the big house, he knew he'd been gone a few hours, long enough for Mulletson to have done bad things to the enslaved mine crew. He quickly cut the dead men down off their mounts, laid them out side by side, then took the stairs two at a time to the front door.

He drew a pistol, and toed open one of the big front doors. It swung in with a long, slow squawk.

22

"Who's there?" The colonel's voice echoed out into the grand entry from his study, off to the right. Slocum didn't respond, just paused, waited for the man to either show himself or go back to whatever it was he was doing in there. The man didn't appear, so Slocum crept forward.

He peered in through the partially open doors of the colonel's office, and for a moment was stunned at what he saw. A panel in the wall behind the colonel's desk was open, the heavy black steel door of a safe swung wide, and inside and atop the desk stood stacks of cash, gold coins, numerous small cloth sacks of what Slocum assumed was gold dust because one was partially opened, as if the man had had his fingers in it. All told, Slocum figured he was looking at a whole lot of money.

"Well, hello . . . Mulletson." Slocum stepped into the room and kept his pistol trained on the florid-faced man behind the desk. "It looks like you aren't so strapped for cash after all. Have you been lying to your men and your investors all this time?"

"You!" The colonel's face reddened even more than it had been, and his beady eyes narrowed.

"Good to see you, too." Slocum gestured at the money. "What have we here? Payroll?"

"Where are the others? Where are my men?"

"You didn't really think they were going to do your bidding, did you? There are three less men you'll have to pay now, you scoundrel. In fact, the only thing they'll ever draw is the devil's wages."

The colonel didn't even blink at the news. "And my gold ore? Is it safe?"

Slocum nodded. "Yep, outside in my saddlebag. Now, get your hat, Mulletson. We're heading to the Pit to take care of this mess once and for all. You are going to finally come clean and answer for everything you've done."

"Slocum, no, we . . . we can't do that. My money! My gold!"

"Who's gold is that? What's that there, on your hands, Mulletson?" Slocum gestured with his pistol.

"What? What are you talking about?" The colonel looked at his hands. "I don't see anything."

"Oh, I see it plain as day. That's blood and sweat, tears and heartache and sadness. That's shame and humiliation. Those are things you can't ever wash off, no matter how strong a lye soap you use. And I am holding you personally responsible for every last bit of it. Now lock up that money because I know some folks who've earned it. They'll be needing it soon."

Surprisingly, the colonel looked at Slocum and smiled. Then he said, "Like hell they will."

Slocum turned too late to see much more than a black blur as something swung down at his head. He collapsed and looked up, his eyesight dimming, his hands strangely not working. There above, looking down at him, Tita smiled, and she was joined by Mulletson, also grinning.

The colonel lifted out his pocket watch and regarded it. "Oh yes . . . the people in the Pit? Those deficients you befriended?" He tapped the face of the watch. "They should all be dead by now." He nodded to the girl, who hit Slocum again.

Daylight blinked out for Slocum.

23

The gunfire began three or four hours after Slocum left the
rim. Eli couldn't be certain just when. But he didn't take it as
a good sign—probably meant that Slocum hadn't been successful and that the colonel had killed him. Or had him killed.
Too damn bad. Eli had liked that crazy cowboy. Kind of fellow you knew when you talked with him didn't pay attention
to the color of your skin, but to who you really were inside,
and to what you were saying.

No matter, because the entire rim had erupted in a rain
of lead, all aimed at the mine entrance. If what Slocum had
said about the colonel's money situation was true, you
wouldn't be able to tell by the amount of lead these boys were
throwing.

Every few seconds, rock chips spattered and stung, stuck
into his arms, his cheeks. So far none had flown into his eyes.

Eli's main concern was for his fellow prisoners. There was
no way he could really protect them, except to keep them hidden in the mine entrance. He returned fire as much as he
could, but their ammunition was limited, and the rim guards,
though a lot fewer than there were a few days before, had
learned from the hard lessons Eli and Slocum had doled out
and had brought over old logs, built up a few earth berms.
Some even crouched behind saddles. All that made it difficult

for Eli to get a decent shot in, but he did return fire now and again just to let them know he was still in the game.

"Eli." Marybeth touched his arm. "It just occurred to me that the reason they're driving us back and keeping us in the mine is because they're going to blow it up with us inside."

"I know, I know," he said, sighting along the top edge of a saddle, then squeezing off a shot. He saw the bullet hit the leather edge, then plow through a tall gray hat just behind. "It don't make sense that they'd blow us up, but that must be the plan. There ain't no other place to go anyhow. We make a break for it and they'll shoot us down like fish in a barrel. I don't know what else to do—do you have any ideas?" He dragged his palm across his forehead and wiped the sweat on his ratty trousers.

Before she could answer, they heard a gagging sound to their right. At the other side of the wide mine entrance, the old man everyone called Cho, an ancient Chinese, collapsed to the ground, a ragged red hole in his neck, blood welling out.

Marybeth ran to him, dragged the man back away from the entrance, but Eli could see the man was dead, or would be in seconds, sure as it snowed in Montana in winter.

"What was he doing up there?" he asked no one in particular. "Didn't he see it was dangerous?" But he wasn't really mad at the man, just sad for him. The old man had been one of his favorite people. Always worked hard, never spoke a word in the entire time Eli knew him, never complained when he had to go without food.

"Maybe he just got tired of it all," said Eli, surprised at himself for sounding so cold and measured about the man's sudden death.

Marybeth closed the man's eyes and did her best to compose him so that the others might not be too upset by the sight of him. "I wish I had seen him, wish I could have stopped him."

"I wish Slocum had been successful," said Eli.

"You don't think he was?" Marybeth looked at him with such worry that Eli immediately regretted having said it.

"I just mean that . . . it's been a while. I expect he's still working that old colonel over a bit, getting us a deal of some sort." He forced a smile, but he could tell she didn't believe him.

"Oh my God," said Marybeth, pointing skyward.

Eli looked up in time to see a stick of dynamite twirling toward them, end over end, its fuse spitting smoke and sparks. It landed thirty feet from the entrance. He licked his lips, threw down the rifle, and snatched up a battered shovel, then bolted out of the mine, straight for the dynamite, its fuse seconds from reaching its end.

"Eli, no!" Marybeth shouted, but there was nothing more she could do. She watched as he reached the stick and slammed at the sizzling wick as if he were stabbing the head off a particularly foul rattler.

No sooner had Eli raised the shovel for one last stab at the wick of the dynamite, then he felt a blazing pain in his back. It wracked through him as if he'd been punched by lightning, but it wasn't enough to keep him from his prize. He dropped to one knee, tossed the shovel aside, and snatched up the dynamite, its half-inch wick barely protruding from the end of the stick.

As he lurched for the mine entrance, his vision began blurring, sounds like thunderclaps seemed to surround him, shouts of familiar voices reached him. The entrance was there, somewhere ahead, wasn't it? His eyes seemed to cross, played tricks on him.

And then he was back in the mine, looked up, and saw Marybeth, that nice woman who could make rattlesnake taste like chicken, then everything went black.

24

"Where am I?" Slocum thought he said it. But his mouth tasted as though it had been filled with gravel and his head filled with more of the same. He opened an eye. Hit in the head, that's what happened. Now he remembered. That damn girl, Tita. He had to keep a sharp eye out for that one. She was a menace.

He tried his question again. "Where in the hell am I?"

"Oh, you're awake, John Slocum. Good, because I need your help."

He forced his eyes open wider, and was pleased to note that he didn't seem to have much of a headache. Must be getting used to being hit from behind, he thought.

"It's you," he said, focusing on Tita. "Damn your hide."

"Now, is that any way to talk to me, John Slocum? I have, after all, saved your life."

"How do you reckon that? Seems to me you tried to take it. More than once!" He tried to sit up and found he was tied, hand and foot, and stretched out flat on his back on the big leather couch in the colonel's study. At least it was padded.

"Untie me. I have to get back to the mine." He looked at her, but she was standing behind the man's desk fiddling with something on the wall. "What are you doing?"

She turned back to him. "I'm trying to open his damn safe.

I know you know the combination, John Slocum. Tell it to me and I'll let you go. Then you can go save your precious friends."

He sagged back against the cushion. "How could I have been so wrong about you? Don't you care about any of them? About Marybeth Meecher? You said so yourself she was good to you, convinced your grandfather to let you dress like a woman."

"Yes, but what I didn't tell you is that she also worked me like a dog."

He looked at her again, trying to decide if the whimper in her voice was for real. It wasn't. She was about to smile, he could just tell. "So please, John, help me and we can go off together. How about that?"

"Where's the colonel? He would have taken his money if he'd left for good."

"He didn't leave for good. He put all his money back in there and locked it in front of me, laughing the whole time, the *bastardo*."

"Tita, where did he go?"

She snorted, shook her head at him. "He kept shouting about his gold, all his gold, how he needed to get it out of the mine right away. He's a pig." She turned back to the safe, then paused and slowly turned back to him.

Slocum watched her face transform from a pleading innocent young woman to a manipulative cat. Her eyes narrowed, her mouth widened into a slight smile, and her tongue tip darted out, ran across her lips.

"Untie me," he said, not taking his eyes from her. "Untie me and I'll help you."

"Help me, then I'll untie you." She glided over to him, lifted her shirt at the waist, and slipped it off over her head.

"What are you doing, Tita? We don't have time for games. Those people . . . they don't have time for this . . ."

He was tied to each end of the couch and couldn't have used his bound hands even if he wanted to. She trailed her long fingers up his thigh and he felt his member respond, thicken despite his anger and determination not to. But it didn't matter. She had stepped out of her skirt and kept dragging her hand along his denims up to his belt. His gun belt, he realized, had been stripped from him. He gritted his teeth and looked away, but the sight of her, massaging herself between her legs with her other hand, her eyes half-open, lids fluttering as if she were in the midst of a dream, it was almost too much to see. Almost.

She unbuckled his belt, unbuttoned his trousers—and then she left him, disappeared behind him. Soon he felt her fingers at his wrists and he wondered if she was going to untie him. Then something cold and sharp touched his wrists. A knife. She held it over his face, smiled down at him, then quick as a flash she sliced through the ropes—but not all the way. He felt them give, worked his throbbing hands, trying to break through the last few strands.

He heard the knife drop, then she came back into view and in another second had freed his stiff member. She bent to it without hesitation, flashing her eyes at him once as her mouth descended on him.

He worked the ropes and he could tell they were nearly ready to snap free even as he watched her silky black hair bobbing up and down on him, drawing on him, and he could feel her teeth just grazing him where it was most sensitive. His breathing slowed, he tried to think of other things, but it was not to be.

He kept working at the ropes as she stood abruptly, then climbed aboard him.

"Tita, please, you know I obviously find you to be a pretty girl. But you are mistaken. There are people who need my help."

"I need your help right now, John Slocum." She smiled at him as she purred the words, and with no hesitation, no buildup, she lowered herself onto him. He would have been a liar if he said it didn't feel damn good, but it wasn't exactly what he had in mind—and then the last of the rope strands snapped.

She ground against him, her head thrown back and her breasts firm, the nipples stiffened, then collapsed down onto him, breathing hard against his chest.

He held his arms above her back and slipped free of the

last length of rope. It proved to be a long one, and he gently took her arms as she made soft sounds of approval, thinking he was trying to prod her into further activity.

But too late she realized he'd bound her arms behind her back. He cinched the rope tight just as she began thrashing and kicking and he just pushed her off him when she almost bit his face.

"Now, now, is that any way to treat the man with the combination to the safe?" He had no idea what the combination was, but she didn't know that.

Her thrashing stopped as quickly as it had begun. "Do you mean you will unlock it for me? For us, I mean?"

"Sure, just give me a second to untie my legs."

"Untie me first, John. This isn't fair."

"Now coming from you, that's funny. I will admit, you are a perplexing thing."

"You say the strangest things, John Slocum."

"Yes, so you said." He buttoned his fly, buckled his belt, and in one smooth motion, flipped her onto her stomach on the couch. She began howling and bucking again and he held her down with one hand at the middle of her back while he tied her feet with the other. It took some doing and he eventually had to rest a knee on her ass so that he could use both hands, but he got her lashed down tight. "Like a roped calf!" he said as he buckled on his guns.

"You don't know the combination to the safe, do you? You *bastardo*!" She looked up at him from the couch, her hair falling in her eyes. She blew at it and cursed a blue streak.

"Now, now, Tita. That's no way for a young lady to talk. Come to think of it, that was no way for a young lady to act." He smacked her once on the backside and winked at her as she thrashed and bucked. He slammed the study door behind him, but her shouts followed him all the way outside.

25

The Appaloosa was still out front, as were the three dead cowboys where he'd left them earlier. He mounted up, then on a whim, he reached back and felt his saddlebag. Flat—no chunk of ore in there. So the colonel had retrieved it—no big surprise.

Slocum clicked his tongue and sank spur as he nosed the Appaloosa into a flat-out run to the Snake Pit, hoping he wasn't too late to help his friends.

It took him the better part of a half hour before he saw the shifting specks in the distance that had to be the remaining rim guards. As they thundered closer, Slocum checked his pistols. Though he missed his Colts, and guessed they were back at the ranch someplace, these would do. They were the ones Everett had worn, but they were in good condition and obviously well cared for. He hoped like hell he wasn't too late.

As he approached, he heard shots and shouting, saw a long black shape that he recognized as he drew closer to the colonel's barouche, though the closer he got, he saw no sign of the white-suited fat man.

Where in the hell could he be? Unless he . . . no, no way he would have gone down there. Still, it was a possibility. Slocum knew the man had gold fever; he'd seen it the way the man had cradled that hunk of ore, just like it had been a new-born baby.

He rode closer, then dismounted and led the horse just east, where the prison wagon stood behind the dozing beasts that pulled it. He draped the Appaloosa's reins over the wagon's front wheel, slid Everett's rifle out of his saddle boot, and still unseen, took a head count.

He saw all the way around the rim now, and counted nine men, most of them on this side. There were a few in prone positions, and unmoving, but he couldn't count them out of the fight. He wasn't sure if they'd been shot or if they were shooters themselves, as various rim guards still cranked out random shots like deadly raindrops into the canyon.

But the thing that interested him most were the two men working the hoist for the basket. They were lowering some-body down there. And if he had to guess, it was the colonel. Gold fever had got the better of him.

From his place of concealment, Slocum dropped down close to the ground, crawled forward, and when he saw one of the near guards rise up and prepare to shoot down into the canyon toward where Slocum knew the mine entrance lay, he let him have it square in the chest. The man whipped upright, then dropped like a stone over the edge. Four more spun toward him, looking for signs of the new shooter, their weap-ons poised.

But Slocum was quicker and he laced three of them, then got the fourth, a man who'd obviously got up on the wrong side of the bed, as he charged at Slocum, growling and yell-ing something about killing him. Slocum waited until the man gained a bit more ground, then cored his forehead with a well-placed shot.

It turned out he was right, and none of the prone rim guards were alive—a good thing, as the remaining four—two of whom had been working the basket mechanism—proved to be tricky to pin down. He managed to wing one, who whim-pered like a struck dog, then wonder of wonders, the other three all looked at one another and shook their heads, seemed to come to some sort of decision. They all threw down their rifles and stood near one another, their hands resting on their heads, angry looks on their faces.

"Where's Mulletson?" Slocum growled at them.

A big, shaggy man who looked and smelled like a buffalo nodded toward the rim. "Just afore you come, he told us to lower him down there. He's gone loco. I'm plumb done with this outfit."

"You bet you are. And any others besides. Now let's go."

It didn't take Slocum long to round up the three, plus their whining, winged comrade, and stuff them into the prison wagon. He used the key that Marybeth had ripped from around Everett's neck when she wrestled with him days before. She'd given it to Slocum before he left the canyon, thinking it might be useful. And she had been correct once again.

"What a woman," he said as he clicked the padlock closed on the prison wagon. Then, just in case one of the men had a key on him, he jammed into the door two steel bars he found under the wagon's seat.

"That should hold you fools for a few minutes."

Then he bolted for the canyon, unsure of what he was about to see when he peered over the rim.

26

A wave of relief flooded over Slocum as he looked down the ropes tethering the basket to see Marybeth waving up to him, smiling and shouting. Despite the fact that her dress was a torn, ragged mess, that her hair hung in her face, and dirt smudged her arms and cheeks, she looked stunning to him. And better yet, all the slaves thronged about her, looking up at him and waving. And many of those gaunt faces were smiling.

They quickly loaded the basket with a handful of slaves and Slocum worked like a madman cranking the massive wooden gear assembly. By the time the first load was topside, he gave serious thought to dragging two of his prisoners out of the wagon to run the thing for him. But he felt like this was something he definitely had to do himself. And so, small load after small load, he brought his friends to the top of the canyon.

The smaller ones made their way to the guards' now-empty camp along the southern end of the rim, and brought back what foodstuffs they found there. The others helped Slocum crank the wheels until, in the last basketload, Marybeth Meecher emerged, smiling, and she and Slocum hugged while their freed friends cheered.

"What about Eli? Mulletson?"

Marybeth's smile faded. "They've gone gold crazy, John. The colonel more so than Eli. But Eli's hurt. He was shot saving us from a stick of dynamite one of these idiots threw down at us."

"Is it bad? Can he walk?"

"Yes, but . . . the colonel's down there with him. In the mine. He walked right by us, acted like we weren't even there. They're both acting strange, John. It's that damned gold."

"I know. Makes men crazy."

"The colonel, he has a gun, and he was carrying that hunk of gold you brought with you. Oh John, when I saw that, I thought for certain you'd been killed."

She hugged him tighter. "It's okay now. But I have to go down there, try to help Eli."

"John, Eli has a short-fused stick of dynamite. The one he saved us from. He kept it. I don't know what he has planned, but I don't think he wants to come back up."

"Oh Lord," said Slocum.

"John, do you have to go down there?"

"What would you do, Marybeth?" Slocum waited a moment, saw her nod reluctantly, and said, "You and the others, lower me down. And wait here for us. We'll be up presently."

He kissed her, then climbed into the basket.

"There is one good bit of news, John."

"What's that, Marybeth?"

She smiled as he disappeared below the rim. "The colonel—he was bit by a snake within a minute after he got out of the basket!"

"Poor snake!" he shouted up at her.

"John, be careful. They're everywhere down there."

He nodded but didn't respond. His mind was on another type of snake.

27

When the basket touched the bottom of the ravine, late-day shadows were drawing large. Slocum wondered how long he had to be down there this time. It was a place he hated, especially so at night. In the lengthening shadows, he clearly saw shapes moving along the ground—snakes. Damn snakes everywhere.

He shucked a pistol and stepped from the basket. Get to them and get out again, at least with Eli. Shoot the colonel if he so much as looked sideways. He stalked across the bottom of the canyon and entered the gloom of the near-dark but familiar mine entrance.

Far ahead, he thought he detected a faint, quivering light. He was right—it was a candle, flickering in the distant gloomy recesses of the mine. With each step, he passed yet another damn rattling snake, until the entire tunnel seemed to vibrate with the serpentine din. The snaky commotion seemed far more extreme than any he'd heard over the past few days as a captive in the deadly little canyon. The odd thought occurred to him that maybe the snakes were angry because all the slaves had gone.

He didn't dare slow his pace, but he kept one hand on the wall to guide him, the other hand held his pistol, and up ahead he heard voices becoming more distinct the farther into the mine he walked.

He rounded one last corner and the near-dark gave way to a sudden honey glow from a reflector candle lamp in Eli's big hand. Slocum held his pistol before him, but neither Eli nor the colonel paid him much attention.

"Mulletson, Eli, let's go right now. The snakes are coming out in big numbers and we have to go!"

Neither man looked at him. The colonel looked pasty and puffier in the face than usual—had to be the snakebite. Eli looked peaked and dizzy. The colonel held a derringer pointed, when he remembered, at Eli. Their conversation was a heated, if halting, argument. As near as Slocum could tell, they were arguing about gold, the damn gold, and that was when Slocum saw the candlelight glinting and reflecting off the vein of pure gold beside the two men. Each had a hand outstretched, caressing the glinting rock face.

The hate in the air was something Slocum could almost touch, and why shouldn't it be? Slave and slaver, both now in possession of a fortune and neither would get it.

Eli's odd gold fever broke for a moment, and he looked at Slocum square in the eye and held up the short-fuse stick of dynamite. Slocum saw for the first time that his friend's shirt glistened, soaked with blood from what must have been his bullet wound.

Eli held up the dynamite and the candle. The colonel weaved and tried to hold up the derringer.

"I'll give you half a minute to get the hell out of here, John Slocum, then I'm touching it off."

"No!" shouted the colonel. "It's my gold! All mine, you . . . you slave! You don't deserve it! I do! I am the only deserving one . . ."

"Eli," said Slocum, one hand outstretched and slowly stepping closer to the two men. "This isn't what you want. We can get you a doctor, plenty of chance for money in the future. We'll look for it together . . . It's what friends do."

The big man smiled at Slocum. "Thanks, but I have all I want right here—more gold than a man could ever spend, and the chance to remove this little speck of evil from the world."

He smiled wider and raised the lantern and the dynamite. "Take care of my free friends up there, you hear? And take care of yourself, friend."

Slocum nodded and tried to smile. Then he pulled in a quick breath, turned, and ran like hell.

For thirty seconds he held his breath.

For thirty seconds he heard the colonel's enraged screams mingle with the hissing and rattling of angry snakes. And over it all rode the big, booming laughter of Elias Jones, free man.

The blast thrust Slocum forward as if pushed by a massive, unseen hand. He sprawled on the ravine floor, rubble raining down on him. When it subsided, he looked back to where the black, gaping maw of the mine entrance had been, and saw only a pile of raw, smoking rock.

John Slocum wiped grit from his eyes and heard shouts from people above. He walked to the waiting basket without looking back.

"Sleep well, Elias Jones . . . friend."

Watch for

SLOCUM AND THE HIGH-COUNTRY MANHUNT

413th novel in the exciting SLOCUM series
from Jove

Coming in July!